Reach for Heaven

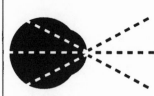

This Large Print Book carries the
Seal of Approval of N.A.V.H.

Reach for Heaven

Susan E. Kirby

Thorndike Press • **Thorndike, Maine**

Published in 1999 by arrangement with
Joyce A. Flaherty, Literary Agent.

Thorndike Large Print® Candlelight Series.

The tree indicium is a trademark of Thorndike Press.

The text of this Large Print edition is unabridged.
Other aspects of the book may vary from the original edition.

Set in 16 pt. Plantin by Al Chase.

Printed in the United States on permanent paper.

Library of Congress Cataloging-in-Publication Data
Kirby, Susan E.
    Reach for heaven / Susan E. Kirby.
       p.   cm.
    ISBN 0-7862-2194-1 (lg. print : hc : alk. paper)
    1. Large type books.   I. Title.
    [PS3561.I667R43 1999]
    813'.54—dc21   99-41719

To Dawn Michelle Kirby,
an expert on brothers

CHAPTER ONE

Mr. Dempster looked up from the application before him and remarked sympathetically, "So you lost both parents in a car accident. What a shame."

Maggie Price accepted his condolences without comment. Seven years had dulled the pain.

"How fortunate you've had three older brothers to look after you," he continued, then glanced down in silence to further study her application.

Maggie let his remark pass uncontested. Small, endowed with large green eyes, a heart-shaped face, and an auburn head of natural curls, she was accustomed to being considered in need of looking after. It was irksome that no one ever suspected it was she who'd done a good deal of looking after not only of herself but of these three robust brothers of hers.

"It's our practice here at Bartlett's to send our nurses' assistants through an eight-week training course before putting them to work," Mr. Dempster said. "And, of course, you will be paid during that training period.

Is that agreeable, Miss Price?"

Maggie assured him that it was, endured another round of routine questions, then, fairly humming with the sweet taste of success, left the hospital on the outskirts of the rural town of Bartlett.

Keyed up to a high pitch, Maggie drove home, home being a dairy farm in southern Wisconsin shared with the aforementioned brothers. At last she was cutting the ties, she thought. On her twenty-first birthday, she'd promised herself she'd seek employment away from the farm and the domineering presence of her three brothers, and, by George, she'd done it! The tie that binds was a nice sentiment. But in her case, it had become something of a stranglehold.

Dashing into the small white frame house that rested in the huge shadow of the dairy barn, Maggie glowed with the news that on Monday she'd be starting her training for a nurses' assistant position at Bartlett's Medical Complex.

James, her eldest brother, grabbed a handful of cookies from the cookie jar, commenting, "Real glamour job, Maggie." He sauntered out of the kitchen, taking some of the sweet taste of success with him.

Yet, noting the proud set of his broad shoulders and black head, she knew instinctively his ego was smarting and she forgave him for being a killjoy. At thirty, he felt proprietary about her. It was hard for him to let go.

Neither did Trent, second of her stairstep brothers, understand this burning need of hers to try her own wings. He remarked, "Nurses' aide is all right for a girl who's underqualified."

"What he means is *unqualified*," Justin drawled, trying to take the sting from his words by lacing a patronizing arm across Maggie's shoulder. "Face it, Maggie. You were meant for apple pie and motherhood."

Maggie flung his arm off her shoulder. "How like the three of you to demean it! It's a very honorable job. I don't care what you say. I'm proud they chose me, and I swear I'll be perfect for the job and I'll love it even more than you three chauvinists love this farm!"

Justin wagged a finger at her. "Motherhood, I'm telling you."

She drew an imaginary line across her throat. "I've had it up to here with motherhood! I've mothered the three of you until you're so spoiled, a featherheaded husband-hunter on the wrong side of thirty wouldn't give you a second look."

"Die-hard bachelors we," said Justin.

"Bachelors, nothing," Maggie flared, not to be humored out of her stand. "You've had it so good, you've never needed the ambition to find yourselves wives. You've been coddled and pampered and picked up after and —"

"In other words, she's through licking our boots," Trent drawled.

"Now, Maggie," Justin said. "If your life's desire is emptying bedpans, then far be it from us to stand in your way."

"Stop belittling the job!" Maggie drew herself up to her full height, which brought her eye to chin with Justin, the shortest of her brothers. "It takes know-how, dedication, and the milk of human kindness, which is something you know nothing about. You're being selfish. You're trying to make me feel guilty because I won't be at your beck and call," she accused hotly, then mimicked, " 'Fix me a lunch, Maggie,' and 'Call the vet, Maggie.' 'Drive to town and pick up that patched tire, Maggie!' "

Belatedly Justin tried to stop grinning. "It's just our way of saying we'll miss you around here."

"Yeah," Trent agreed, then proceeded to show his true colors. "Are we going to have any supper around here tonight?"

"Not unless you fix it yourself!" Maggie

stamped through the living room, where James pulled her to a halt.

"Cool off, Maggie, and consider this. How about if I offer you a regular monthly wage instead of an allowance?" he said, perfectly serious.

"Grrr!" Maggie went on to her room and slammed the door hard.

"Guess that means no," James said. "I'm afraid she's serious about this, boys."

Maggie Price set about proving her seriousness. For the next eight weeks, she poured all the attention she'd previously lavished on her brothers into learning how to be the best nurses' assistant she could possibly be. In October she passed the course with flying colors, which impressed none of her brothers half so much as the yield they were getting on their corn crop.

"Could be the Cordell harvester," James was saying to Trent over dessert the evening she announced her impressive test score.

"Did you hear me?" Maggie belligerently withheld the second slice of pumpkin pie James automatically reached for. "I said I got the highest score out of a class of twenty-seven students in Madison."

"Nice, Maggie," James said sincerely enough to get his piece of pie. Turning to

Trent, he resumed their conversation. "That combine picked the field nearly clean."

"Didn't even leave much grazing for the cows," Trent said.

"It was a nice straight stand of corn," Justin pointed out.

Maggie felt like screaming. "Out of twenty-seven, Trent," she said as she left the table to fill the cup Trent had shoved her way. "Aren't you going to congratulate me?"

"Well, after all, sis, what's to know?" he said. "There's a limited number of places to stick a thermometer."

Swelling up like a poisoned toad, Maggie wondered why their approval had been important to her in the first place. *She* knew it was a job needing qualified and caring people. That was what mattered. Still, she could not resist a retort.

"Should you choke on that coffee, Trenton Price, don't expect *me* to clear your windpipe!"

She took her place at the table again and tried to eat her dessert, which had somehow lost its appeal.

Justin took up the teasing where Trent had left off. "Don't they teach you how to slap choking folks on the back at nurses' aide school?"

"Nurses' assistant," Maggie informed him haughtily. "Aide is outdated. And," she added, "a careless slap might not save Trent *should* he happen to choke."

"Hate to disappoint you, sis, but I don't intend to choke," Trent said and snickered.

"More's the pity." She started clearing the table.

Out of the three, Justin was the only one who possessed even a twinge of sensitivity.

He drummed up enough interest to ask, "So when does this job of yours officially start?"

"Monday."

"Monday?" James groaned. "Our bookkeeper is coming Monday. I was counting on your being here, Maggie."

"Recount, James, because I won't be."

"Darned inconvenient," James muttered. "I'll be glad when you get this whole silly Florence Nightingale notion out of your system."

"Wait'll she loses her first patient," Trent chortled. "She'll come home, cry her eyes out, and never go back."

"What a horrid thing to say!" Maggie snapped.

"And hoping I'll choke is nice?" he countered.

They glared at one another, both equally

quick of temper, equally slow to back down.

Justin hopped up and uncharacteristically grabbed a dish towel.

"Why don't I help you dry, Mag? Top out of twenty-seven, huh? That's using your noggin for something besides a curl mop." He tugged playfully at a curl.

She turned her back on Trent and accepted Justin's show of interest as sincere. Maybe there was hope for Justin, after all.

CHAPTER TWO

Maggie wasn't long on the job at Bartlett's Medical Complex when she discovered putting all she'd learned into practice was trickier than filling in answers on a test sheet.

Yet under the guidance of Nadine Perkins, the registered nurse in charge of the surgical ward to which Maggie had been assigned, Maggie struggled along. She was too much in awe of the woman to fail.

Mrs. Perkins, Maggie was told, was team leader on their ward. Her instructions were to be followed promptly and to the letter. It was natural that Nadine would evoke respect and obedience.

Yet Nadine with her miss-nothing blue eyes and her severely cropped head of iron-gray hair moved Maggie past respect to reverent fear. Nadine could get more reaction out of Maggie with an uplifted eyebrow than any of her brothers could with an hour of haranguing.

Somewhere in the middle of her second week, Maggie relaxed a little and fell into the hospital routine. The job was demanding, yet she found it satisfying, and time seemed to pass very quickly.

On Wednesday afternoon Maggie was putting fresh sheets on the beds vacated by check-out patients. One of the beds was in the same room with Mr. Jenkins, a sweet old man Maggie had taken very much to heart. After she finished with the bed, she stood back and regarded it with a critical eye.

"A ladybug couldn't hide under that there sheet," the elderly Mr. Jenkins commented. She flashed him a smile of gratitude, and he asked, "I can't hear that blasted contraption. Tune it in, will you, honey?"

Maggie increased the volume on his TV set, accustomed by now to his inability to master the television controls. Half a smile still gracing her lips, she breezed into the next room and nearly collided with a tall man who seemed to materialize out of nowhere.

"Excuse me," she murmured, sidestepping her way around him to see he was not alone in the room. He had for an entourage one complaining young woman, unfamiliar to Maggie, and a frosty-eyed Nadine, who was finishing up the customary forms.

"Are you allergic to any drugs?" Nadine was asking him.

"I have a reaction to penicillin," the man told her.

At his low, smooth, familiar tone of voice,

Maggie gave him a startled second glance.

Her heartstrings gave an unexpected tug. Yet his gray eyes slid over her face with no returning start of recognition.

But why would Cole Cordell recognize her? Maggie asked herself as Nadine continued to question the man. Soundlessly she went about the task of making the recently vacated bed, recalling her one meeting with Cole Cordell, the man she secretly adored. Was it six months ago? And even then, he'd spared her no more than cursory attention.

The bulk of his attention had been given to showing her and her three brothers around the Cordell Harvester, Inc. farm-implement factory that had been started by the senior Coleman Cordell as a risky family venture.

She'd felt like a tag-along on that occasion, yet she had, to her own surprise, found it a memorable afternoon. The efficiently run assembly line, which turned out one Cordell harvester combine every half hour, lingered in her memory less clearly than did the dynamic personality of Cole Cordell.

It had surprised Maggie at first that a man of Cole Cordell's seeming importance would play the role of tour guide. Yet his workers took it in stride, which led her to assume it was a common practice of his.

And perhaps it was a good policy, she had mused.

It had impressed James, Trent, and Justin. Shortly thereafter, they'd purchased a Cordell harvester. These thoughts and others flashed through her head as Maggie put the finishing touches to the bed and tried to melt out of the room without attracting any attention.

"Just a moment, Maggie," Nadine said, thwarting her attempt. "Mr. Cordell is scheduled for an appendectomy in the morning. Would you please make him comfortable?"

Nadine left the room and the young woman with Cordell transferred her complaints to Maggie.

"We specified a private room." Her haughty look raked Maggie over. "Can't something be done about this? Surely you have one private room available."

"If we did, I'm sure Mrs. Perkins would have shown you to it," Maggie said with an unprofessional stir of Irish irritability.

"This is ridiculous." The young woman swept a strand of ash-blond hair over her shoulder and tapped an impatient foot. "Cole isn't some nobody off the street. He *owns* Cordell Harvester. He surely rates a private room, even in *this* out-of-the-way place."

Maggie found the girl's sardonic emphasis of certain words annoying. "The second bed is unoccupied," she pointed out. "And since I'm not staying, I guess you could call this private."

"You needn't be impertinent," the young woman snapped.

Her attention straying to Cordell, Maggie didn't reply. A slanted smile lifted one corner of his mouth to reveal even white teeth.

"I'll take the bed by the window, if it's all the same to you," he said.

His female companion didn't appear to like the smile that passed between them. Taking Cordell's arm, she said, "The Madison Hospital would have seen to it you had a private room."

"That'll do," Cordell said and prepared to unpack his suitcase.

Maggie pointed out the closet to him, politely suggested he change into his pajamas, and, on her way out, indicated where the bathroom was.

"Wait!" he called out to her, and Maggie paused while the young woman interrupted him yet again, trying to persuade him to change his mind about staying at Bartlett's.

"Kirsten, it's my appendix," Cordell informed her in exasperation. "If I want to part company with it here, I guess it's my business."

"Your risk, you mean," she argued. "Madison would have been more convenient, among other things. You won't get much company in this out-of-the-way place."

"Which suits me just fine. I want to get this over with and back to the plant. Women! Want to turn everything into a blamed social event."

"Present company excluded," Maggie murmured, delayed from flight by his arresting gray gaze. He seemed uncertain how to take her remark, so she said, "We can provide you with a 'No Visitors' sign if you wish."

"I might, at that."

"If there's nothing else . . ." Again, Maggie attempted to leave.

"How long will I have to stay here?" he asked.

"You'll have to ask your doctor," Maggie told him. "I couldn't say."

"Of course, she can't," the woman chided. "For goodness sake, Cole! Read her pin. She isn't a nurse."

Cordell took a step nearer. "Maggie Price. Price?" With a puzzled frown, he thought a moment. "Name's familiar."

Her heart missing a beat from the intensity of his alert gray eyes, Maggie opened her mouth to speak of the tour she and her brothers had taken those long months ago. Yet he stopped her with an uplifted hand.

"Don't tell me. I'll think of it. I never forget a name."

"Nor a redhead," the young blonde said with venom.

Cole Cordell laughed. Brittle and self-mocking, it seemed an unpleasant sound.

The man continued to consider Maggie. "I wouldn't call her hair red, exactly. It's deeper than red. Like an oak leaf in autumn," he clarified.

Maggie, who seldom blushed, felt a slow warmth creep up her neck as she scurried down the hall away from Cordell and his woman friend, who was clearly very stuck on herself.

Yet as Maggie went about her varied tasks, Cole Cordell kept irritatingly popping to mind. Still, it wasn't until she reached home that she mentioned him to anyone.

"*The* Cole Cordell?" James asked as he lounged at the kitchen table while she put the finishing touches on a hastily prepared meal.

"Of Cordell Harvester, Inc.," she said.

"Why would he come to a hospital like

Bartlett's?" Trent asked.

"To get his appendix removed," Maggie said dryly, putting a plate of cold roast beef on the table.

"But why Bartlett's?" James insisted. "A Madison hospital would have been more convenient, it appears to me."

"Maybe he heard Bartlett's had the best-looking nurses' aides — assistants," Justin said, winking at his sister.

"The way I hear it, Cordell has a woman picked out," James said. "If you'll remember, when Cordell's father died, his will made a ripple in the news. He left the Cordell plant to Cole, but he left a fledgling firm, a by-product of the harvester plant, to his stepdaughter. Her name escapes me at the moment."

James fell silent and bit into the beef sandwich he'd made.

Justin picked up the ball and kept the conversation rolling. "If you read the social page, James, you'd remember Kirsten Fontana is the lady's name. And if you can judge by her pictures, she's quite a dish."

"*You* read the social page?" Trent asked his younger brother.

"No." Justin grinned. "I just look at the pictures. Hers caught my eye. Blond and leggy. Good-looking. And when I glanced beneath the picture, saw an announcement of her engagement to Cordell, I was doubly interested. It turns out she's Cordell's stepsister, and heir to the small-equipment firm."

James whistled low. "I figured that Cordell for a businessman through and through. If you have to marry, may as well marry with your own best interests at heart."

Maggie felt a sharp pang. "So he's married," she murmured.

"Not yet. Christmas, I believe, was the date," Justin informed her.

Her appetite waning, Maggie toyed with her food, the name Kirsten echoing in her head. Why, that was the snooty young woman who'd been with Cordell today! She dropped her fork with a clatter.

"Say, you aren't a little sweet on the guy, are you, Maggie?" Justin asked.

Maggie wadded up her paper napkin and tossed it at him. "I've scarcely spoken to the man."

"Cordell was the man who led us on that tour, wasn't he?" Trent said. "Yeah! And we were all so surprised a guy on the top rung of the ladder, so to speak, would take the time."

"Of course, it was Cordell," James said

and, as they ate supper, the three men called to memory that afternoon of six months ago.

Maggie did some mental backtracking of her own. Seeing Cole Cordell pacing that hospital room today had been something of a shock after entertaining thoroughly childish daydreams of him for six months. She couldn't help the silly daydreams. He was so suave, good-looking, soft-spoken, but with a commanding edge of authority.

She'd noticed that and much more about him that single afternoon those long months ago. She'd remembered the side part to his smooth, thick dark hair, the even, sun-browned features that accented the grayness of his eyes. All in all, he had a lot going for him. And it had irritated her at the time that she'd fallen victim to the disgustingly common (not to mention totally irrational) ailment of love at first sight.

Like a twelve-year-old with a bad case of puppy love, Maggie had trailed Cole Cordell through the factory that day. He'd scarcely noticed her, so busy was he explaining the workings of the assembly line to her brothers.

And so he was to be married. Christmas. As good as signed, sealed, and delivered. Maggie sighed deeply and pushed her plate away. Miss Snooty Kirsten was right. Cole Cordell should have gone to Madison for surgery. It would have been a lot easier on her.

Then again, maybe not. Maybe a little exposure to the man would be the perfect cure for this adolescent crush of hers. She'd been worshipping him from afar, so to speak, creating an exciting imaginary picture of this man she did not know. Now was her chance to discover he, like her brothers, had flaws. And that would surely be the cure for her ludicrous infatuation.

One of Cole Cordell's flaws became apparent the next morning. Maggie had just clocked in when Nadine sent her to answer a call from room 101.

Cole Cordell, it seemed, was subject to presurgery jitters the same as any other flesh-and-blood mortal.

He worked up a smile as she entered the room.

"Were you needing something, Mr. Cordell?" Maggie inquired, returning the smile.

"Just some company. It occurs to me I might drift off to sleep and never wake up. Be that the case, I want a witness to the fact I did it most gallantly."

Catching a glimpse of vulnerability

25

helped her not at all. It seemed rather a heartwarming flaw. And thinking such, she offered soothing assurances that he would be just fine.

"How long before the operation?" he asked.

Maggie glanced at the watch on her slender wrist. "Not long now. Just relax."

"Easy for you to say." He grew silent, then asked, "Has Kirsten arrived?"

"Your fiancee? Yes. She's waiting in the lounge. If you'd like, she could come in until they take you to surgery."

Shaking his head seemed an effort almost beyond him at this point. "She'd make a fuss," he objected. "I hate fusses."

"Me too." They exchanged another smile and Maggie knew with a sinking feeling she was losing ground fast.

"I remembered your name, why it was familiar. Last night, after Kirsten had gone." He frowned. "But it's gone from me again."

He seemed annoyed, not realizing it was the presurgery medication he'd been given that impaired his thinking.

Maggie helped him out. "My brothers and I toured your factory a few months ago. You acted as our guide."

That didn't seem to click with him, for he asked, "You farm?"

"My brothers do. And, I might add, they bought a Cordell harvester shortly after our visit to your factory."

"Smart boys," he said. "The factory! Yes! You were there too."

Maggie nodded. He fell silent for a time, though his eyes never left her face. Covertly, she studied him too. His face was very tan against the white sheet, tan and full of character. Dark brows crested over arresting gray eyes. Faint laugh lines fanned out from his eyes.

He had a nice, even mouth, closed now to hide equally nice teeth. His hair, straight and fine where it fell across a lightly creased forehead, missed being black by several shades. And though freshly shaven, he carried a shadow that suggested a heavy beard.

In drugged fascination he studied her face. "You have a freckle on your lip."

Maggie nodded, her finger rising to the upper right corner of her lip. His eyes closed. Maggie started to walk away.

"Is Rhoda still here?" he asked her.

Knowing nothing of this Rhoda, Maggie didn't try to answer. Nadine chose that moment to poke her head in and, in a hushed voice, give her a list of duties.

In a morning flurry of bathing and feeding patients, Maggie squeezed in a prayer. She was gratified when news came Cole Cordell was out of surgery and in the recovery room.

Some time later, Maggie saw a practical nurse on soft-soled shoes go into his room.

Unable to contain her concern any longer, Maggie asked Nadine, "How did Mr. Cordell's surgery go?"

"Routine." Nadine turned from her desk to request a patient's chart from Alice, the ward secretary.

"He seemed rather nervous about the surgery. I'm glad there were no complications," Maggie said.

Nadine gave her a sharp look. "I wouldn't concern myself too much with Mr. Cordell. The man is a born survivor."

Feeling the reprimand had been unwarranted, Maggie started to walk away. Perhaps Nadine thought she was shirking her duties, asking questions when she should be working.

Nadine stopped her with a softer tone. "He tends to leave a trail of casualties in his wake, Maggie, so take a word to the wise. Keep your dealings with him entirely impersonal. He's a womanizer."

"Yes, ma'am," Maggie murmured.

"You're thinking if it had been old Mr. Jenkins who you asked after, I wouldn't have given it a second thought," Nadine said. "Isn't that right?"

That had been her thought exactly, but she didn't confess it, so Nadine continued.

"But, Maggie, Mr. Jenkins isn't a highly successful businessman whose bachelorhood has turned a flock of feminine heads. You're getting a good start here at Bartlett's. Don't mess it up, getting emotionally involved with Cole Cordell."

Abruptly, Nadine turned away, saying, "Speaking of Mr. Jenkins, he's requesting help adjusting his television again. And Miss Smith in 105 needs assistance getting to the bathroom."

Tucking the patient chart under her arm, Nadine clipped off down the hallway. Cheeks flaming from the head nurse's reprimand, Maggie glanced at the ward secretary to see how much she'd overheard.

Enough, it seemed. "Don't mind Nadine," soothed the freckle-faced Alice Owens. "She's an excellent nurse and generally very fair-minded. But she has a blind spot where Cole Cordell is concerned."

"I guess!" Maggie muttered. "Someone might have warned me."

"When we get off work, take time for a cup of coffee with me and I'll fill you in," Alice suggested.

CHAPTER THREE

After Maggie had collected the lunch trays, she took a water pitcher into Cole Cordell's room. She noted at a glance his complexion was far more pale than it had been that morning, yet he was resting easily.

Kirsten Fontana sat in a corner chair, flicking through a fashion magazine. She spared Maggie no more than a brief nod. Maggie paused to admire several lovely bouquets of flowers that had arrived, then quietly set the pitcher of water on the bedside table.

Cole's eyes fluttered open.

A smile framed Maggie's lips of its own volition. She asked softly, "How are you doing?"

"I guess I lived."

"A minor miracle, in this place," Kirsten said from her corner.

Cordell grimaced. "She disapproves of your hospital on the prairie here," he managed in a weakened voice.

A defense of Bartlett's seemed pointless. Maggie said nothing.

He whispered, "Get rid of her and I'll take you to lunch."

"I would," she teased, "but I've had lunch."

"Lucky you."

Kirsten rose from her chair and came to his bedside. "He still possesses enough life to be a tease." In a waft of expensive perfume, she leaned down to drop a kiss on his cheek.

As if she owns him, Maggie thought, jealous. She scurried off to freshen other water pitchers, then returned to the nurses' station. Alice gave her a winning smile.

"Would you watch the station just a second? I'm suffering from caffeine withdrawal. A cup of coffee is a positive must."

Laughing, Maggie assured Alice she wouldn't let anyone walk off with the place. Alice had no more than stepped around the corner when a man approached the station.

Trim, mid-thirties, gray-spattered dark hair waving back from his face, the gentleman had that air of authority she'd come to associate with doctors.

His step abounding with energy, he took her in at a glance. "Maggie Price," he said, reading her name tag. "You're new, aren't you?"

Maggie said that she was. Without introducing himself, he turned his back on her and reached for a chart.

The light from Mr. Jenkins's room flashed, and he glanced up from the chart to direct her, "Why don't you get that?"

There was a vague unease in the back of her mind, yet she lacked the confidence to point out she was temporarily watching the station. After all, he was a doctor. She surely could not defy him.

When she returned from supplying Mr. Jenkins with an extra blanket, the man was gone. Alice was back at her desk, and Nadine was in evidence too.

Maggie thought she detected a bit of tension in the air, yet when Nadine spoke, her manner was calm. It was Alice's silent accusing glance that troubled Maggie.

The afternoon passed in a blur of chores her two hands were hard pressed to perform quickly enough. Yet she thrived on the bustling atmosphere. Not for a moment would she have traded her new job for an afternoon of carrying out farm errands.

When three o'clock rolled around, Maggie clocked out, grabbed her pale blue sweater and pocketbook, and hurried to the snack bar where Alice soon joined her.

"You're lucky I don't wring your little neck," Alice said without preamble as they sat at a corner table.

"Me?" Maggie's eyes widened. "What have I done?"

"I thought you were going to tend the station for me while I fetched myself a cup of coffee this afternoon," Alice accused. "When I came back, Nadine was puffed up like a thundercloud and you were nowhere to be found."

Maggie gasped. "Did I get you in trouble? Alice, I'm sorry." Hurriedly, she tried to explain to her new friend what had happened.

"I was waiting for you to return when one of the doctors came to the station to get a chart. Mr. Jenkins's light flashed on, and the doctor told me to go check on him. It never occurred to me he'd leave before you returned."

A frown clouding her pert, open face, Alice asked, "Which doctor was it?"

Maggie shrugged. "I'd never seen him before and he didn't introduce himself. But he was of average height, mid-thirties, I'd say. His hair was dark, but touched with gray, and he wore it in a center part, I think. His eyes . . ." She squinted, trying to remember. "They were blue, I believe."

With furrowed brow, Alice commented, "Doesn't sound like any doctor I know."

Remembering her earlier stir of unease, Maggie worried aloud, "Well, I just assumed he was a doctor."

"The rule is, we aren't to leave the station unattended," Alice said. "So naturally, Nadine was cross with me."

"Gee, I'm really sorry," Maggie apologized again. "Perhaps if I explained to her how it happened —"

"No, just let it go," Alice said. "Nadine is a little on edge of late. Personal problems, I believe."

They fell silent as the waitress approached. Maggie ordered apple pie and Coke, and Alice wrinkled her freckled nose.

"Just coffee for me." To Maggie, she added enviously, "It must be nice to be able to afford all those calories."

Relieved Alice wasn't going to remain disgruntled with her, Maggie turned the conversation to more general avenues. When their order came, Alice sipped her black coffee, then chuckled.

"You have to toughen up, Maggie. When Nadine jumped on you over Cole Cordell, you looked like a little whipped pup."

Now that it was over, Maggie could laugh at herself. "Did I? I should have a thicker hide after all the dressing downs I've taken from those brothers of mine. But I'll admit it. Nadine intimidates me."

Alice chuckled. "You aren't the only one.

Perhaps it goes with the job. She has to be in command, to be able to maintain control. Still, she'll go to bat for her nurses and she is respected by one and all."

"She's very dedicated," Maggie murmured.

"Yes. Her job is very important to her. Next to her son, Wade, I'd say her job is the most important thing in the world to Nadine."

"She has a family?"

Alice nodded. "Her husband is dead, but she has Wade, her son. And Wade has a child." She sipped her coffee. "Wade's wife left him recently, taking their baby girl. And Nadine's taking that rather hard."

"What a shame!"

"It's all rather a mess," Alice agreed. "And Nadine, being so responsibility oriented, has trouble accepting the fact her son is cut from a different mold. He's rather a weak man, which I'd guess is the reason he's lost not only his wife and child in recent weeks, but also his job with Cordell Harvester."

"Cordell Harvester?" Maggie echoed.

"Yes. And that's where Nadine's professional shell of uninvolvement is being strained to the limit. You see, Cole Cordell and Wade's wife were childhood sweet-

35

hearts. It came as quite a surprise to everyone, especially Cordell, when Rhoda up and married Wade Perkins three years ago."

Maggie twirled her straw in her Coke, feeling a little stunned. Cole Cordell had resided in a special corner of her mind for months now, a complete stranger who stubbornly defied eviction. Yet he'd been only a shadow. Now he was taking on shape and dimension, and she thought of him more and more.

"So there are hard feelings, I take it," she said.

"With Nadine, I'm sure that's true," Alice told her. "However, I doubt Cordell is even aware Nadine is Wade's mother. Talk has it once he'd adjusted to Rhoda and Wade's marriage three years ago, he was very decent about the whole thing. So you can't say he at that time was harboring hard feelings. He even gave Wade a good job in management at the plant."

"So he isn't a grudge-holder," Maggie said, thinking that at least was in his favor.

"Apparently not. But I'm not sure his move was a wise one," Alice confided. "Wade is the small-minded jealous sort. I gather he felt a lingering resentment toward Cordell, despite the fact he'd won the girl and landed a good job on top of it. Something brought it to a head a few months ago. Cordell fired Perkins and shortly thereafter, Rhoda filed for divorce."

"Mercy!" Maggie pushed her pie aside. "Sounds like a regular soap opera. Where does Kirsten Fontana fit into the picture?"

"Cordell's stepsister, turned fiancee?" Alice questioned. "A good point in Cole's favor. If there was anything to the rumor Cordell still carried a torch for Rhoda, I doubt he'd have gotten himself engaged to Kirsten just when Rhoda made moves to free herself from Wade."

Maggie didn't risk a comment. The whole mess blew her fairy-tale illusions of Cole Cordell into mass confusion.

Alice prattled on quite happily. "A man like Cordell is bound to attract a lot of feminine attention. I mean, what a prospect! He's good looking, quite charming, they say, and he owns a thriving business. I'd sure give him a whirl, if he gave me a second glance."

She sighed. "Let's face it. When you're approaching thirty, there aren't that many eligible bachelors around."

"You?" Maggie echoed, disbelieving. "You're thirty?"

"Fast approaching it." Alice drained her cup.

And, as Maggie fumbled with her pocketbook, a brilliant idea dawned on her. A little matchmaking might be cheering enough to get her mind off Cordell. Considering her brothers, it would be more than cheering — it would be downright challenging!

"Would you like to come out to my place for dinner tonight, Alice?" she ventured innocently.

"If my kitty-cat can watch the tube without me, I guess I'm free. What time do you want me?" Alice reached for the check as the waitress deposited it on the table, but Maggie snatched it up first.

"My treat. Come about six."

Alice slipped a tip under her coffee cup. "Want me to bring something?"

"Just yourself. It should be an interesting evening."

Alice exhibited passing suspicion. "If we're going to milk cows, count me out. I'm terrified of any animal bigger than myself."

Maggie laughed. "We won't go near the cows, I promise. There are other interests at my house," she added mysteriously.

"Such as?" Alice challenged.

"Come at six and find out," Maggie teased.

James was openly annoyed. "I'll eat early,

then get out of your way, if it's entertaining you're into now."

Maggie stamped an impatient foot. "You'll do no such thing. You'll eat at the table with the rest of us. And you'll not scowl at my friend either. You'll scare her to death. She's a gentle soul." She turned to include Trent and Justin. "If it isn't too much trouble, the three of you could change into something a little less tacky than tattered flannel shirts and faded jeans."

"My tux is at the cleaner's," Justin teased, then halted her temper tantrum before it could take flight. "But I think I can hunt up a presentable pair of slacks and a sweater. Would that make you happy?"

"Blissfully," Maggie muttered. Here she was going to the trouble to introduce them to a really super girl, and did she get one ounce of cooperation? She did not!

"I'll bet she has a face like a horse," Trent predicted as he and Justin retreated from the kitchen.

"She does not!" Maggie shouted after them. "And the two of you had better be polite too, or you'll be eating jelly sandwiches for the next six months!"

To James, she complained bitterly, "You'd think I could invite a friend to dinner once in seven years without it being such an imposition on the lot of you."

Annoyingly intuitive, he warned, "Just so long as there aren't any matchmaking ideas dancing around in that curly head of yours."

"Me?" She adopted an expression of complete innocence. "I've said it before. You three are a lost cause. I wouldn't waste my time."

Still, she set the table for five, the clink of cutlery accompaniment to her cheerful humming. She planned that Alice would sit beside her, facing her three brothers across the table. Surely one out of the three would realize Alice was vivacious, attractive, and good-hearted. Yes. It ought to be an evening interesting enough to chase Cole Cordell from her mind.

CHAPTER FOUR

Trent and Justin came in from milking at five-thirty, allowing themselves just enough time to clean up for dinner. James was not as cooperative. He hadn't yet shown when six o'clock rolled around.

"What's keeping James?" Maggie fumed. "Alice will be here any minute."

"He said he'd wash up the equipment and clean out the barn by himself." Justin reached for a carrot stick on the relish tray.

"You may have to drag him in with a rope," Trent told her. "He wasn't looking forward to meeting this friend of yours." He too swiped a carrot stick.

Maggie resecured the plastic wrap over the relish tray and shook a wooden spoon at them. "You two stop nibbling. I want something left when Alice comes." Resuming her work at the stove, she asked, "Would you go see what's keeping James, Justin?"

"No use rushing him, sis. He'll be along when he gets hungry." Justin went to the window and pulled the starchy white curtain aside.

"Does your friend drive a green Vega?"

41

"Oh good. She's here." Maggie bustled around the kitchen, issuing last-minute orders. "Trent, get an extra chair out of the back room, will you?"

"Say, she isn't bad." Justin sounded surprised.

Trent elbowed him aside and chimed in, "She *is* nice looking. Maggie, why didn't you say so in the first place?"

"I did! And you two country bumpkins quit gaping out the window. The folding chair, Trent," she scolded. "And, Justin, do get James, won't you?"

"Why look up more competition?" Justin replied, then amended, "Go after him, Trent. I'll get the door."

Trent was equally disinclined to go after James. Maggie was debating whether to go after him herself when Justin ushered a laughing Alice into the kitchen.

"This guy says he's the butler. Is that right?" Alice asked Maggie, her eyes twinkling.

Maggie wagged a finger at Justin. "Don't believe a word he says. He's a big tease." She went on to introduce both of her brothers to Alice.

While more reserved in his welcome than Justin, Trent appeared every bit as much interested in Maggie's friend. Maggie's hopes rose. Maybe these brothers of hers weren't so uninterested in women, after all. Maybe James kept them so involved in farm work, they had no time to get out there and look!

Alice took a deep breath and sighed contentedly. "It smells heavenly in here."

"My aftershave, no doubt," Justin quipped.

And not to be outdone, Trent put in, "Cow Pasture's his brand."

Alice's laughter rang out, a light musical sound. "Let's give credit where it's due. It's Maggie's roast I smell. I'm starving."

"Then we'll eat," Maggie decided aloud, keeping her annoyance over James's absence to herself. As she put the last of the dishes on the table, her seating arrangement went awry. Trent and Justin took a place on either side of Alice.

Throughout the meal, they good-naturedly vied for the lion's share of Alice's attention, but Alice showed no partiality. All in all, Maggie was hard pressed to remember when dinner had been any more fun.

She'd nearly forgotten her annoyance with James until he came through the kitchen door, still dressed in faded work clothes, a day's growth of beard, and boots that were anything but clean.

43

"Did I miss supper?" he asked.

Maggie paused in the cake-cutting to introduce her oldest brother to Alice. James gave the freckle-faced girl a swift, thorough glance, nodded in her direction, then took his place beside Maggie.

As he began to fill his plate, conversation resumed again. Yet Maggie felt a vague strain that had not existed until James's arrival.

Alice seemed more subdued. Slanting a measuring glance in James's direction, she said, "Maggie tells me you have a dairy herd. How many cows does it take to make a herd?"

Seeing the question was directed at him, James replied, "In our case, forty-eight."

"Is that a lot of cows?" Alice asked.

"Not really." James pushed his chair back from the table. "I'll have coffee and cake in the living room, Maggie."

"It would seem like a lot if you had to milk them by hand," Justin said, trying to cover James's abruptness. "But everything is modernized. With the pipeline milking system, we can do the milking and clean up in an hour, hour and a half."

Maggie served the cake, then took James his requested portion. In a whisper, she called her oldest brother to task. "That was very rude. Alice isn't a farm girl."

"I hate it when women ask questions just to be yakking."

"She wasn't. She was interested," Maggie said.

James said, "Your Alice has the undivided attention of Trent and Justin. I don't guess she needs me hanging on her every word too."

Noting the uncompromising jut of his jaw, Maggie said, "Thank goodness Justin and Trent show a few manners."

With that she pivoted and returned to the kitchen. Maggie ate her own dessert in silence, puzzling over James's behavior. Why had he set his face against Alice when he scarcely knew her?

When all that remained of dinner was a table of dirty dishes, Trent and Justin tried to persuade Alice to take a tour of the dairy barn.

"I think I'll pass," Alice told them. "I'll help Maggie with the dishes."

Remembering her friend's earlier claim to a fear of farm animals any larger than herself, Maggie told her brothers, "Alice doesn't want to go, boys, so leave her alone. We're going to do the dishes and, unless you want to help, clear a path."

They weren't *that* eager to monopolize

Alice's every minute. Both boys joined James in the living room, leaving Alice and Maggie to enjoy a private visit.

"Why didn't you tell me your brothers were so handsome?" Alice demanded in a lighthearted voice. "Just look at me! Jeans and a sloppy shirt. I would have dressed more enticingly, had I known."

Maggie chuckled. "Clothes don't make the woman. They like you just the way you are."

"Two of them like me," Alice corrected. "James took an instant dislike." A pretty pout shaped her mouth.

"James has been out with the cows too long," Maggie remarked and they both laughed. After hanging up her dish towel, Maggie ushered Alice into the living room.

Justin and Trent turned away from the television set to join Maggie and Alice in hospital shoptalk. James maintained an attitude of complete boredom whenever they tried to draw him into the conversation.

Yet before the evening could bog down, Justin suggested, "Why don't we drive into Bartlett? There's a good picture playing at the theater."

"Sure," Trent chimed in. "We could all go."

"That does sound like fun." Alice

46

beamed. "It's a double feature, isn't it?"

Maggie groaned. "Count me out. I have to work tomorrow."

"I don't," Alice sighed. "It's my day off. So how about it, fellas? Shall we?"

Justin and Trent needed no further persuasion. They were at the door when Alice turned to check with Maggie one last time. "Sure you won't change your mind?"

Maggie shook her head and Alice glanced past her to James. "How about you, Jim?"

The shortening of his name earned her a contemptuous, "Nope," from James, who scarcely glanced away from the market report on the television screen.

"Spoilsport," Maggie accused James.

"Never mind," Alice said. "We'll get along without him. Come on, Maggie, go with us."

Knowing her rising hour would be an early one, Maggie refused to change her mind. Justin latched onto Alice's arm.

"I'll ride into town with you, Alice. Trent can follow us in the pickup. That way after the show, you won't have to come back out here to get your car."

"Fine," Alice agreed. She thanked Maggie for the meal, then linked her free hand through Trent's arm. "Let's go, fellas. The evening's young."

Sandwiched between them, Alice made her exit. As soon as the door closed behind them, Maggie scowled at James.

"Nice going, James. You get the prize for the most boorish behavior."

"Thanks," he replied, unruffled.

Arms akimbo, Maggie declared, "Alice probably went away thinking you were a real jerk."

"I can live with it." James rose from his chair, switched off the television, and patted Maggie's head. "I warned you not to play matchmaker."

"I wasn't!"

His face a map of disbelief, he said, "Come now, Maggie. I might have been less suspicious if she'd been homely. Or if she'd been less of an operator — parading out of here with Trent and Justin hanging to her side like a couple of wet pups."

He crossed to the door, yanked it open, and walked out into the darkness beyond.

"So you *did* think she was pretty!" Maggie chortled.

"Give it up, sis," he called back to her. "I've got my life in order and have no intentions of messing it up with a woman."

What a terrible attitude! Maggie slammed the door, closing herself into the restful quiet of the house. The evening had had its moments. But with Trent and Justin gone and James out at the barn, time hung heavy on her hands.

Whimsical thoughts of Cole Cordell floated temptingly to mind. Maggie tried to shut out the memory of his gray eyes searching her face as the sedative had made its effects known.

She wished she hadn't listened to Alice's gossip, wished a shadowy illusion of his old sweetheart Rhoda didn't rise up to taunt her. She wanted badly to think he had nothing to do with the separation of Rhoda and Wade, Nadine's son. Yet thoughts of Cole marrying the haughty Kirsten in December were disagreeable too.

Face it, Maggie thought with painful honesty. You've fallen hard for a guy you don't even know. And what's more, he doesn't know you're alive unless you're standing over him with a thermometer in your hand.

He was in a class far removed from the simple world of Maggie Price. Having faced the pointlessness of entertaining further daydreams of Cole Cordell, Maggie went to bed.

The next morning she awoke depressed. Even in her dreams, Cole Cordell eluded her, turning away to stroll off into oblivion with a woman shrouded in mystery. Rhoda

Perkins? she mused as she dressed for the day. Was that the faceless woman in her dream? Odd this Rhoda should haunt her, rather than Kirsten Fontana, who was such an obvious roadblock to any furthering of a relationship with Cole.

Impatient with herself, Maggie shrugged it all aside. Reaching for the stars was foolish. Especially when you stood five foot two in your stocking feet, she thought, with a twist of humor, and tied her shoes.

It was Maggie's practice to prepare breakfast while the men milked. Often she had to leave it warming in the oven. That was the case this morning. The men had not returned to the house when her departure time neared.

Curious to know how Trent and Justin's evening in town had gone, Maggie shoved plates of bacon strips and scrambled eggs into the oven, grabbed her purse and jacket, and ran out the front door.

There was a tangy scent of frost to the October day. Maggie shivered against the cold dark morning and slipped on her jacket as she hurried down the well-worn path to the big barn.

The barn with its stone foundation rising to meet clapboard siding was very well kept. It came first with James, for a sound barn was a necessity to the care of the dairy herd. The kitchen door could and did squeak like a crazed mouse, but the latch on the barn door was well-oiled and opened soundlessly at her touch.

James was alone, moving the cows into position for the morning milking.

"Where's Trent and Justin?" Maggie asked.

His scowl spoke volumes. "In bed would be my guess."

"In bed?" Maggie echoed. "Are they sick?"

"Tired is more likely." His face was accusing. "Which might have something to do with the hour they crept in last night — rather, this morning."

He crooned to a white-faced cow in a tone far gentler than the one he used on Maggie, "Get along there, Bess."

Maggie backed out of his way. "I guess they're entitled to a late night once in a while. They'll survive."

"I'm sure they will," he growled in a wilting tone. "But in the meantime, what am I supposed to do for help?"

"Do to them what you'd do to me — yell them out of bed."

He made no comment, which led Maggie to believe he'd rather have them come running out late, guilty-faced for oversleeping.

"You must have made a dandy army sergeant, James," she remarked. "Unfortunately Trent and Justin and I need a little breathing space. There's no harm in rest and recreation once in a while."

James said nothing, just kept moving the cows into place.

Maggie shifted from one foot to the other. "If you want me to wake them, speak now or forever hold your peace. I have to get moving, or I'll be late for work."

"Perish the thought," he said, his voice disagreeable. "You know you've disrupted everything around here, first with your whim for an outside job. Now you're working to make Justin and Trent discontent.

"We have a farm to run, Maggie. You used to understand how, with the narrow margin of profit in agriculture, everyone has to pitch in and do their part."

"James!" she protested. "I haven't dumped tea in the ocean! I'd simply like an income of my own. As for the boys, they had one late night out in how many months? You're overreacting."

Maggie turned on her heel and stomped to the door.

"What kind of girl goes out with two guys

at the same time, for crying out loud?" he shouted after her. "Is that the kind of friends you're making on this new job of yours?"

"You're positively Victorian!" Maggie snapped at him. "Not to mention you're behaving like a sorehead. Alice is a nice girl." She tamped down her irritation and took a wild guess at the true reason for his irritability. "After all, Alice did invite you along too. It was your choice to decline."

Ignoring his thundering reply, Maggie dashed for her car. She was turning the key in the ignition when Trent and Justin ran out of the house, buttoning flannel shirts as they ran.

Justin gave her a cheerful wave as he passed toward the barn, but Trent leaned in her open car window.

Pulling a worried face, he asked, "Is James mad?"

"A little growly, yes. But don't go in apologizing. You boys are entitled to a little fun now and then. Who knows? Maybe it'll be contagious and he'll take a night off. Working like he does, he'll be an old man before his time," Maggie predicted. "Sometimes I think he already is — in his reasoning, at least."

Changing the subject, she asked, "How was the movie?"

"Great. And Alice is pretty terrific too." Trent grinned cockily. "She tried not to show favoritism, but just between you and me, Justin doesn't stand a chance."

Trent sauntered off toward the barn, whistling off key, and Maggie pulled away, chuckling to herself.

CHAPTER FIVE

Through the course of the morning, Nadine's instructions sent Maggie scurrying in and out of Cole's room on more than one occasion. But it wasn't until afternoon that Maggie had a chance for more than a few brief words with the man who had so unknowingly infiltrated her heart and soul.

Acting on Nadine's instructions, Maggie entered his room to ask, "Mr. Cordell? Could I persuade you to go for a walk? Perhaps as far as the patients' lounge and back?"

Cole accepted her company with a welcoming smile and allowed her to help him on with his robe. But once on his feet, he refused the arm she offered, saying, "I'll make it under my own head of steam, thanks."

Maggie fell into step with his painstaking pace. "You're doing very well," she murmured. "How are you feeling?"

"Like talking about something less depressing than how I feel."

Maggie grinned. "Go ahead and growl. You won't scare me. You aren't even the first grouch I've tangled with today."

"Oh?" he questioned. "Who might hold that dubious honor?"

"My brother, James," Maggie told him, her steps faltering as he came to a stop.

"And did you get him subdued?"

His grin did strange things to her heart. Unable to match his gray-eyed gaze, Maggie focused her attention on the long hallway before them.

Falling in step with him again, she admitted, "I took the easy way out. I came to work."

"Wish I was at work," he muttered through clenched teeth. "Six weeks off, at least, according to my doctor. I'll go crazy with nothing to do."

"We have a ward for that too."

He grinned at her again and her heart tripped way out ahead of the creeping pace of her feet.

"Shall we go back?" she asked when Cole paused for a second rest.

"And have you think I can't make the grade?" He shook his smooth dark head. "Never. It's patients' lounge or bust."

Shoulders squared at a determined angle, Cole resumed his cautious pace. Maggie was glad when the lounge loomed before them. With one complete wall of windows, the lounge was a room of sunshine, and by unspoken agreement, they moved toward the windowed wall. The horizon beyond was a breathtaking display of autumn-hued aspens, maples, oaks, and birch. Dressed in reds and golds and deep browns, the trees surrounded a small lake beyond the hospital property line.

Maggie watched him stare out the window, his face a study of gloomy impatience. Sympathizing with his hemmed-in feeling, she murmured, "It won't be so long a time, Mr. Cordell. You'll mend in time to rake a few leaves off your lawn."

A smile emphasized the grooves framing his mouth. "I was thinking of leaves, but not of raking them. See the oaks by that outcrop of rocks?"

Maggie followed the direction of his pointing finger. "I see the rocks, but I'm not certain those are oaks, not from the distance."

"Sure they are. They stand out from the others. And the leaves are that rich brown with only the faintest hint of red."

"All right," Maggie conceded. "I'll take your word for it. So they're oaks."

His hand brushed her hair lightly. "Those leaves are the very color of your hair."

Pleased, yet embarrassed too, Maggie

quipped, "Likened to a tree. Now that's a first. An oak tree at that. I certainly don't tower though," she said, laughing as she stretched to achieve her full five feet and two inches of height.

"No, but you stand out from the rest."

Uncertain how to respond to his seemingly casual remark, Maggie studied the trees in silence.

Unexpectedly, he nudged her and added:

"Of course, some varieties of oaks are prickly and shaggy too. That's why they stand out."

More at ease beneath his teasing grin, Maggie exclaimed, "Heaven forbid I should be prickly or shaggy. But even that would be better than a hemlock. Rumor is they're poison."

He laughed and moved a little closer, until his arm brushed hers. "So pick a tree. What would you wish to be likened to?"

"A willow, I think," Maggie decided after a moment's thought. "I'd like to think of myself as being flexible, like a willow."

"If it amuses you, go ahead," he said. "But you strike me as too strong-willed for a willow."

"Strong-willed as in stubborn?" Maggie questioned. "Stubbornness runs in my family, I'm afraid. My brothers are all stubborn too. Especially James. He's the world's worst!"

"James as in the grouch?" he asked, and she laughed. "I remember your brothers as a group from the factory tour, but I can't recall them as individuals. Which one is James?"

"He's my oldest brother," Maggie told him. "James had just finished his tour of duty in the army when my parents were killed in an auto accident. I was fourteen at the time, and a couple of my aunts were determined I was going to come live with them.

"James wouldn't hear of it. He and Trent and Justin worked very hard to maintain a solid family atmosphere that would satisfy the social worker who came around once in a while."

Maggie sobered, remembering the pain of the time. Yet it was a pain laced with the pride of accomplishments too. James had kept the family together, and she'd played an important role in that.

"Your brothers sound like men I'd like. I'm sorry I'm so hazy on that meeting at the factory." He lightened the moment with a crooked grin. "Truth is, it was you who captured my attention."

"Ha!" Maggie shook a finger at him.

"That's flattery if ever I heard it. I suppose you think you can sweet-talk me into fetching a wheelchair so you won't have to walk back to your room."

He adopted an injured expression. "You aren't taken in by my easy charm?"

"Hardly! I had a far different impression of that day, Mr. Cordell. You were completely absorbed with explaining the workings of the assembly line to my brothers," she informed him. "The only notice I got was from some old codger on a forklift. And the only reason he noticed me was he nearly mowed me down!"

Laughter radiating from his eyes, Cole remarked, "You get a guy on incentive pay at Cordell's, put him on a forklift, and you've got a lethal weapon."

"I'd say! And the forklift driver wasn't the only fella in a hurry. All your workers were busy as a hive of swarming bees. My brothers were very impressed."

His smile indicated his pleasure. "We have a good group at Cordell's. We try to treat them fairly and they respond by working hard."

With quiet pride, Cole spoke further of the work at Cordell's. It wasn't hard to guess he was satisfied with the business as his life's work.

Maggie remarked as much and he replied:

"I'm satisfied, I guess. At times it would be nice to be less tied down by it all. But I learned early in the game if you expect your employees to work hard, you must do the same. Otherwise, they lose respect. And then there is a lot of discontent."

"Is that why you mingle out on the floor with them?" Maggie wondered aloud.

"Show people around, you mean?" he questioned and she nodded. "No. That's just something I enjoy doing from time to time."

"Good customer relations?" Maggie guessed, and he laughed.

"You figure all the angles, don't you?" Cole commented as they started back toward his room. "What about you? Have you worked here long?"

"This is only my second week," Maggie confessed. "Does it show?"

"Only in that you aren't very good at hiding your sympathy."

"I didn't know I was supposed to," she replied, a little annoyed with his teasing smile.

"Sympathy is a dangerous thing. It can bring out the cry-baby in a patient," he told her. "Even a grown man."

"You don't strike me as the cry-baby sort."

"Don't I?" He crooked an eyebrow at her. "I'll bet if I whined around, you'd get me that wheelchair for sure."

"You're wrong there, Mr. Cordell. In the first place, Mrs. Perkins said you need the exercise, and in the second place, I'd sooner step out in front of a train than disregard her orders."

His grin faded. "I was wondering about Mrs. Perkins. Do you know her well?"

"Not really. Why?"

"A man by the name of Wade Perkins used to work for me. I was curious to know if she was related to him."

"Wade is her son, or so the ward secretary tells me," Maggie said.

"You haven't met him?"

Uneasy over his close scrutiny, Maggie replied, "No. Why?"

"No reason, really. I was merely curious to know whether he ever came around the hospital. Perhaps to see his mother?"

"If he does, we haven't been introduced as yet." Troubled by his dark look, Maggie persisted, "Why do you ask?"

"It sounds so crazy, I hesitate to mention it." He glanced down at her, then quickly away. Entering his room, he muttered, "Must have been the sedative."

"What?"

He paused a long moment, seeming to size it all up in his mind. "I thought Wade came into my room yesterday. It seemed he even spoke to me."

"You know him well?"

Cole nodded.

"Then perhaps he came to visit you."

"No." His voice was grounded in certainty. "He and I aren't on visiting terms."

Maggie waited until he was comfortably settled in bed before turning to leave.

"Hey," he objected. "Don't run off."

"Did you need something else?"

"Just some sympathetic company."

His entreating smile was hard to resist, yet Maggie hardened her heart. "You aren't the only patient on this ward, you know," she told him lightly. "Turn your television on, or the radio. Or take a nap."

He glowered at her with mock severity. "If you're set on abandoning me, then at least promise you'll be my leaning post again tomorrow."

Maggie laughed at him. "You didn't need me today. By tomorrow you'll be skipping down the halls. Besides, tomorrow is my day off."

"That'll be one long day," he complained.

"I think you'll survive," Maggie said dryly.

But as she left his room, a rosy glow colored her world. One look at Nadine moments later brought back a reminder of the head nurse's warning — "He's a womanizer."

Her glow fading, she wondered, Was he? Was Cole Cordell merely filling in his boring hospital hours with a little harmless flirting? If that was the case, it didn't say much for the man's integrity. He was engaged to Kirsten Fontana, despite how unengaged those gray eyes of his looked as they smiled into hers.

Maggie drove home that day, realizing that away from his mesmerizing smile it was easier to be cautious, logical about the matter. And pure logic told her Cole Cordell was a dead end as far as she was concerned. He traveled in a circle foreign to her own. He was city. She was country. He had money. She did not. She had simple values as to what was good, fair, and honorable. She wondered, in the light of his casual attitude toward Kirsten, his betrothed, if he had any values at all.

But through the course of the following day, a day of catching up on baking, laundry, and errand running, Maggie found it impossible not to think of Cole.

If only she could consider him a harmless

passing fancy! Like her old skis, roller skates, and outmoded clothes that cluttered the closet, he was cluttering up heart-space. Someday, someday soon, she'd have to do some heart-cleaning! She'd make a discard parcel of him, similar to the bundle the thrift shop received after a week of spring cleaning.

But until then, she decided to enjoy whatever attention he bestowed upon her, and Kirsten Fontana would have to look out after herself!

On Saturday, Maggie noted a flurry of secretive whispering as she approached the nurses' station. That often was the case when the night shift brought the first shift up to date on all that had occurred in the past eight hours.

With her watch showing a few minutes until seven, Maggie ran a comb through her hair and touched up her lipstick.

"Big trouble!" Alice muttered. Catching Maggie's arm, she pulled her off to one side. Her pert features animated, Alice went on in a voice kept low, but feverish with drama.

"There was a mix-up last night. Cole Cordell was running a fever. A bit of infection, they surmised, and he was given a shot of penicillin."

"But he's allergic to penicillin!" Maggie cried in alarm. "Is he all right?"

"Yes, now he is. But he gave the night staff a good scare. He broke out in hives, was having breathing difficulty, and . . ."

Listening no further, Maggie started toward room 101.

Alice dashed after her. "Stop, Maggie. You don't want to go in there!"

She grasped Maggie's arm and used her size advantage to pull her to a halt. "It isn't your place to go barging in there. Anyway, Miss Fontana is pitching one royal fit. She's determined to pack him up and move him to a hospital in Madison."

"If he's had a rough time in the night, he's in no shape to be moved!" Maggie cried.

"Calm down!" Alice pleaded. "Nadine is in there now with Dr. Kanton and Mr. Dempster. They're telling him that very thing. To go bursting in there would be to lay your job right on the line."

Maggie's determination to see Cole and know he was indeed all right wavered. She demanded of Alice, "How could such a thing happen? They must have known he was allergic to penicillin. It had to be on his chart. I heard him mention it to Nadine the day he checked in."

"Nadine filled in his papers, it's true."

"And what about his doctor?" Maggie demanded, scarcely listening to Alice's reply. "Wasn't his doctor consulted before they gave him the shot?"

"Dr. Watts had left for a long weekend and couldn't be reached," Alice told her. "One of the staff doctors on duty made the decision."

"Without consulting his chart?"

Alice lowered her voice to a hoarse whisper. "It wasn't on his chart."

"But it had to be! I heard him tell Nadine myself, I tell you!"

Alice shook her head, eyes darting nervously around, then resting on Maggie again. "Maggie, it wasn't. Nadine insisted she made the notation. But if she did, then someone came along and changed it."

"Tampered with a chart?" It took Maggie a moment to comprehend what that could mean. "Without proper authorization, it would be very difficult to get hold of a chart."

"They're strictly confidential, it's true," Alice agreed. "And yes, it would be difficult. But not impossible." Alice took her arm and drew her back toward the nurses' station. "A man of Cole Cordell's standing is sure to have made an enemy or two along the way to the top."

"Then they believe it was done purposely? That someone intended him grave harm? Even . . ." Wide-eyed, Maggie did not finish her sentence.

"It looks that way," Alice told her with a grave nod of her head.

"Unless Nadine got careless and is merely covering up for her mistake," Maggie reasoned.

"That doesn't sound like the Nadine *I* know," Alice disagreed. "Her own sense of fair play would not allow her to keep silent if she, as you are suggesting, merely made a mistake."

But what if it wasn't a mistake? Maggie wondered, a horrible thought taking root. Could Nadine have done it purposely? Could she be harboring such a grudge toward Cole Cordell for firing her son that she would spurn her sacred duty of saving lives and plot to end one instead? Maggie pushed the thought away. No. Not Nadine, surely!

"Hurry up," Alice urged. "It's almost seven."

Maggie returned to the nurses' station with Alice where the third shift was finishing up last-minute duties. More than one pair of eyes shifted down the hall to room 101 as the door burst open and Kirsten

Fontana, cheeks ruddy with temper, flounced out.

"Cole is checking out," she told them. "Make whatever arrangements are necessary while I go down to admissions and sign release papers. And you'd best have him ready by the time I bring the car around. I don't like being kept waiting."

As she walked down the long corridor, one of the younger nurses giggled nervously. "Hop to it, girls. Her majesty spoke."

A ripple of laughter broke off as Nadine, Dr. Kanton, and Mr. Dempster appeared in the hallway. The two men went in pursuit of Miss Fontana. But Nadine turned in at the station to issue a string of curt orders. The night shift soon departed and the morning routine went smoothly into gear.

Conquering her timidity where the head nurse was concerned, Maggie approached Nadine to ask, "Is Cole Cordell leaving?"

"It appears that he is." Nadine snapped her mouth shut in a stern line.

Maggie swallowed hard. "A man of his position — it's rather a black mark for Bartlett's, isn't it?"

"Worse than that! He could well sue. He will, if Miss Fontana has her way. She's pressing for an investigation into the 'slipshod manner in which Bartlett's conducts business as usual,' " Nadine spewed out, quoting Kirsten's haughty voice and manner.

"Is there any hope of changing Cordell's mind?" Maggie asked, knowing she was inviting a rebuke from Nadine. Yet her luck held. Nadine did not choose to put her in her place.

"It seems not," she said. "Mr. Dempster promised he'd move heaven and earth in an effort to come by an explanation for the mistake. But with Miss Fontana screeching, 'Criminal negligence!' I don't believe Cordell comprehended a word any of the rest of us spoke."

"Maybe if I talked to him —"

"You?" Nadine interrupted, her eyebrows shooting upward. "What makes you think that would alter matters?"

"Perhaps it won't. But it wouldn't hurt to try." A slow warmth crept into Maggie's cheeks. "He and I seemed to find common ground the other day. He might listen."

Nadine ran a shrewd eye over her, then dismissed her with a shrug. "Go talk to him if you like."

Maggie hurried down the corridor to room 101. She opened Cole's door and caught her breath, her heart lurching with misgivings.

Cole sat on the side of his bed, pale, exhausted, grim of mouth. A shadowy blotch of hives was still in evidence along his neck.

At the sound of her light step, he turned his face toward the door and summoned a bleak grin. "Fine friend you are. Take one day off and they nearly kill me."

A pair of socks dangled from one hand. He ran the other hand across his haggard, unshaven face and complained, "I can't seem to reach my feet. Want to help me here?"

Maggie crossed the room and snatched the socks away. "You're in no shape to go anywhere."

"I'm alive, as Kirsten so profoundly pointed out. And eager to stay that way."

"Then lie back down and let Mr. Dempster handle this matter."

"Can't do that. Kirsten's booking me a hospital room in Madison. She'll be back to get me any minute and, in her present frame of mind, won't much appreciate my pokiness."

Maggie studied him and subtly changed tactics. "You disappoint me. I didn't tag you as a man who let a woman do your thinking, Cole."

"Cole, is it?" His dark-shadowed eyes flickered over her. "Since when did you drop the very proper 'Mr. Cordell'?"

A slow flush crept up her neck as she endured his scrutiny, wondering what her chances were of changing his mind.

When she did not reply, Cole covered a yawn and grumbled, "Just forget the socks and hand me my shoes. I wonder what's keeping Kirsten?"

"It'll take a while for her to check you out. There are papers to be filled out."

"Papers?" he questioned, his voice heavy with irony. "That's a joke. What do they do, fill them so they can file their mistakes? Is that the purpose of all these papers they so diligently insist upon?"

"Cole, it was an accident," Maggie said quietly. "At least, it would seem it was, and if that's the case, then I'm the first to understand your misgivings. Still, I wish you'd give us a chance to iron it all out."

" 'It would seem it was'?" he quoted. "What is that supposed to mean?"

Having said more than she'd intended, Maggie ducked her head and tried to divert his attention with a new argument. "What do you have to gain, checking out of here so tired and weak you can't put your own socks on?"

"Don't try to sidetrack me. What did you mean, 'It would seem it was an accident'?" he demanded.

Maggie hesitated a long moment, wondering how much trouble she would be getting into, repeating what Alice had said. But if indeed his life was in danger, shouldn't he know?

"Perhaps this is off base," she began on a note of uncertainty, "but could it be that it wasn't an accident? Could someone who knew of your allergy have taken steps to have that notation erased from your chart? Do you have any enemies? Any clever enough to get to you here in the hospital?"

He was quiet a minute, then, neither confirming nor denying the existence of enemies, said, "That's pretty farfetched."

"Then forgive me for asking." Stepping around him, Maggie fluffed his pillow and made one last effort. "Won't you lie back here like a nice fellow? I give you my word you'll be in the best of hands up to the very minute you walk out of here."

"Yours?" His eyes roamed her features.

Uncertain whether she was being teased, Maggie assumed a bantering tone. "Among others."

"Are you taking a sacred oath to stand guard over me?"

"If I do, will you stay?" Maggie countered.

"Maybe I will." Dark sooty eyelashes

flicked down over sleepy gray eyes. "It's an interesting proposition." Dropping back on the pillow, he continued. "I would like to know, though, why you've gone to such pains to persuade me."

Thankful for the flippant reply that came so easily to mind, Maggie grinned. "Because in two weeks I haven't lost a patient. I wouldn't want you to be the first, which well could happen if you go bouncing over the pothole-infested road into Madison."

"In other words, you're madly in love with me and can't bear to see me go." A faint twinkle lit his eyes, and she laughed.

"Whatever feeds your ego. It's starving, that's plain to see." Maggie ran nervous hands over the sheet in a straightening motion. "So I can tell Mrs. Perkins you're staying?"

"Only if you finish tucking me in, tell me a story, and give me a good-night kiss."

"You really are a baby!" she accused, pulling the covers clear up to his chin.

"When it suits me," he confessed. "Now for the story."

Maggie spared a moment's thought. "Once upon a time a young businessman had his appendix —"

"Handsome young businessman," he interrupted.

"Don't interrupt! Where was I? Oh, yes. Had his appendix removed at Bartlett's Medical Complex. He was a model patient for a week, then went home to live happily ever after. The end."

"I didn't specify a fairy tale, but that'll do." He smiled lazily. "That's two out of three. I believe you owe me a kiss."

Maggie backed away from the bed. "And I'll go on owing it. You wouldn't want me to get suspended for getting too friendly with the patients, now would you?"

"Who's to know? I certainly won't tell."

Noting the glint of devilment in his eye, Maggie backed off another step. "And if Miss Fontana were to poke her head in the door?"

"Kirsten and I understand one another perfectly," he said.

Maggie had no wish to hear about Kirsten. Yet she knew the difficult woman had to be faced with the news he was staying. Waiting for the inevitable storm, Maggie emptied his hastily packed suitcase, watered his fresh flowers, and straightened his bedside table.

"If you're withholding the kiss, you can go," he said when she made no move to leave. "Kirsten is going to come flying in here with fury in her eyes, and you don't want to get caught in the middle."

Maggie straightened her shoulders. "I don't mind staying."

"I'd rather you went."

Maggie asked, "You're sure?"

He chuckled. "I won't change my mind about staying, if that's what's worrying you. Go and give Mrs. Perkins the word I'm staying. Of course, I'm expecting a lot of special attention to make up for that shot of penicillin," he warned.

"Nadine doesn't play favorites," Maggie said, and he grinned.

"It isn't her special attention I want."

CHAPTER SIX

Kirsten didn't take the news any better than Maggie expected her to. Her high-heeled staccato echoed down the hallway. She sped past the nurses' station, shot Maggie and Nadine a poisonous look, then disappeared down the corridor.

Nadine had taken Maggie's news that Cole was staying with no outward show of gratitude. Maggie wisely omitted his bid for special attention. Yet whenever his light flashed, Nadine was quick to send Maggie.

Cole's color improved through the course of the day, and the hives faded. By the time Maggie's shift ended, he was prowling the halls in a disgruntled mood.

Heading her off as she came out of Mr. Jenkins's room, Cole requested, "After you clock out, come back to the patients' lounge, will you?"

"Only for a minute," Maggie agreed. "I have to run into Madison before I go home, so I can't tarry long."

"Have a heart, Maggie. I'm bored to tears. And, besides, I want to ask a favor."

A little wary of Nadine's reaction, Maggie

waited in the coffee shop until Nadine had gone home for the day. Only then did she return to the patients' lounge.

Cole was glowering out the window. He turned as she drew near and accused, "I thought I'd been stood up."

"By your guardian angel? Never."

Cajoled into a grin, he asked, "Where have you been?"

"Getting a Coke in the coffee shop."

"You might have invited me along."

"You aren't allowed off this ward."

"And you wouldn't bend the rules for me?" He looked hurt.

"No," she replied in an adamant tone.

Cole went to the nearest table, sat down, and toyed with the partially worked jigsaw puzzle in front of him.

"You mentioned a favor," Maggie reminded him.

"Are you in a hurry or something?" he asked, glancing across the table at her.

"A little. And also, I'm curious."

Trying to force a piece of puzzle into a place of similar shape, he began, "It occurs to me I'm going to need a driver when I check out of this place the day after tomorrow."

"Kirsten won't come after you?" Maggie took the piece from him, her eye on a more likely space, and fit it snugly into place.

"Kirsten doesn't like it when her word fails to become law. She's washed her hands of me for the moment."

Welcome news if ever she'd heard it. Keeping her face averted, Maggie reached for another puzzle piece. "And you know of no one else who would pick you up?"

"It isn't a simple matter of picking me up from the hospital. I won't be able to drive for a while and I've just begun to realize how badly I detest being immobile," he said, grimacing as he tried to force yet another puzzle piece where it did not belong.

Maggie took it from him. "So you're looking for a driver. Sorry to say, I can't think of anyone offhand." She put the piece neatly in place. "Though if you're willing to wait until my shift ends Monday, I'll run you home."

"I doubt that'll be necessary," he told her. "I'll phone the Madison paper and place a want ad for a driver."

"With such a temporary job, you may not find any takers."

"It won't hurt to try," Cole said rather blandly. "Unless of course you'd like the job."

"Don't be silly. I have a job." Maggie found places for a handful of puzzle pieces before it occurred to her to offer, "But if you'd like, I'll take the piece into the Madison paper for you, since I'm running into town anyway. I have to pick up a part at the implement dealer's for James. Which reminds me, I better get going. The place closes at five-thirty."

Maggie took a notebook from her purse and passed it over to Cole. He scribbled the "help wanted" ad and handed it back to her. Maggie frowned as she read it aloud.

"You're willing to pay *that much* just for a driver for a few days? Maybe I'll give your offer another thought."

He laughed off her comment, yet it was to Maggie one more reminder that they were worlds apart. It would be foolish to think his money made no difference. She and James and the boys scrimped and saved and just got by, while people like Cole threw money around ever so casually.

It wasn't something Maggie wanted to think about, her world being so different from Cole's. So rather, she passed the miles into Madison mulling over the events of the day.

Had someone tampered with Cole's chart? And if so, hadn't it been a terrible risk? While Alice was correct in saying it wouldn't be impossible to get a chart, the fact remained it would take careful planning with a little luck thrown in. And at best, it seemed a long shot, for who could have predicted Cole would be in need of an antibiotic following his surgery?

It was a confusing muddle. Replaying it over in her mind made Maggie's head hurt. Nadine seemed the only obvious suspect. While she would have had easy access to the chart, it seemed so out of character, not to mention a gross overreaction to Cole's firing her son.

Further, it seemed unlikely Nadine would dare risk her own secure position at Bartlett's by doing so foolish a thing. Not unless she was slightly unbalanced where her son was concerned. And Nadine, with her stern commanding way, seemed about as well balanced as anyone Maggie knew.

So who did that leave, assuming the chart had been tampered with? Wade Perkins himself, perhaps? Alice had mentioned Wade was jealous where Cole was concerned, never convinced Cole wasn't lurking in the wings to retrieve Rhoda from the confining bonds of matrimony.

And was Cole? Maggie's thoughts shifted course as she approached the Madison city limits in the fading afternoon light. Fearful of the outcome, Maggie shied away from that particular question.

After dropping the advertisement at the newspaper office for Cole, Maggie picked up the part James had ordered, then fought rush-hour traffic through the center of town.

On impulse, she pulled into a fast-food chain and ordered fried chicken to-go. It would be a treat not to have to cook for the men, Maggie thought as, with the cardboard box of chicken under one arm, she began to push open the glass door.

A man coming in held the door for her. As Maggie smiled and nodded her thanks, something about him struck her as familiar. But when no stir of familiarity touched his returning glance, she decided she was mistaken.

A few steps further on, Maggie nearly plowed into Nadine Perkins. "Why, Nadine!" Maggie said with a smile. "I didn't expect to run into you here in Madison."

A brief twist of Nadine's mouth passed for a smile. She returned Maggie's greeting, then hurried inside. Puzzled at the woman's reaction, Maggie climbed into her car and pulled out of the parking lot into the busy flow of traffic. Two stop lights further on, the man's familiarity hit her like a bolt out of the blue.

He was the man from Bartlett's! The man she'd assumed to be a doctor! The man who'd reached for a chart, then sent her off to check Mr. Jenkins! She'd yet to see him around the hospital again. And Alice hadn't been able to identify him from her description.

Suppose he wasn't a doctor. Suppose the chart he'd held in his hand was Cole's and he'd sent her away so he could change a few vital pieces of information!

And wasn't it a huge coincidence Nadine had been following that particular man into the restaurant? Too huge, it was! Abruptly, Maggie braked and turned right, earning an irate blast of car horn from the vehicle behind her. Intent on knowing if Nadine had been with, rather than merely behind, the man, Maggie drove back to the restaurant.

It wasn't necessary to leave the car. As she circled the parking lot, she caught a glimpse of Nadine through the glass window. Seated with her at a small table was the man from the hospital. They appeared to be arguing — that is, if their gestures and taut facial expressions counted for anything.

Maggie considered breezing inside again and casually stopping by their table to see if she could get an introduction without being too obvious. A moment's debate cast doubt on the wisdom of such a plan. Perhaps she was being ultra-cautious, but it seemed unwise to make it obvious to the man she'd recognized him.

It didn't take a genius to figure out he must be Wade Perkins. Had he really gone to Cole's hospital room that day? Or had Cole dreamed it? It seemed very possible it had not been a dream, but reality.

But before she went to anyone in authority, Maggie wanted to make a positive identification. Vowing to call Alice the moment she arrived home, Maggie wove her way through traffic, finally reaching the country road that led home.

The glow of Maggie's headlights shone on Alice's green Vega as she pulled into her drive. Glad she and Alice could work it out in person rather than over the phone, Maggie hurried inside.

Alice helped her set the table and fix a salad to go with the chicken. Maggie relayed how she'd unexpectedly run into Nadine in Madison, hurrying the story along while she and Alice were alone.

Giving a loose description of the man with Nadine, Maggie asked, "Would that be her son, Wade?"

Alice frowned as she took rolls from a

package. "It sounds like him. Why?"

"Remember the day Nadine got angry with you for leaving the station unattended?" Maggie asked.

"The day *you* left it unattended," Alice corrected.

Conceding the point, Maggie asked, "Do you also remember the man I described to you? The one I thought was a doctor because he sent me to see about Mr. Jenkins?"

Alice nodded. "Why?"

"Because he was the same man I saw with Nadine."

"Wade Perkins?" Alice yelped. "Maggie, are you thinking what I'm thinking?"

"That Wade Perkins is the one who changed Cole's chart?" Maggie said. "What better explanation? You told me yourself he harbors a grudge against Cole, so there's his motive. And it appears he made the opportunity, thanks to my stupidity."

"It really wasn't your fault, Maggie," Alice said kindly. "Thinking he was a doctor under those circumstances was a natural mistake."

"It becomes more and more clear Wade Perkins was up to no good that day. He may have even gone into Cole's room. Cole thought he did, but later dismissed the vague memory as a dream, induced by the drugs."

Before she could say any more on the subject, Justin poked his head into the kitchen, asking, "Are you two fixing dinner or carrying on a gab session?"

Maggie had intended to keep quiet over the Cole Cordell matter, but when Alice unwittingly spilled the whole story to her brothers, Maggie went on to explain how Wade Perkins tied into things.

Justin teased her over dessert. "Are you turning detective now, Maggie? Isn't one job enough?"

"Maybe she has something personal at stake." Trent winked at Justin and made a guess. "Maybe she's sweet on Cordell."

Only James took it seriously. "I don't like the sound of this, Maggie. If this Perkins fellow is responsible, he isn't going to take kindly to your turning him in."

"What else can I do?" Maggie asked. "Cole Cordell could have died from the shot of penicillin. Wade Perkins can't be allowed to get away with that!"

James sipped his coffee. "If it was Perkins, you might be putting yourself in danger by informing on him. The man sounds a bit ruthless to me."

"And if I don't inform on him, he might do something else to harm Cordell," Maggie argued. "And just imagine how I'd feel if that happened. I'd be responsible by my silence."

"I wasn't suggesting you keep quiet about what you know," James told her. "Just that there might be a better way to handle it."

"How?" Justin questioned.

James scraped his chair back from the table. "By telling Cordell what you know. He struck me as a fellow who could look after himself."

"But he's just had surgery!" Maggie pointed out. "It'll be a while before he has his strength back. How can he be expected to protect himself against any future attempts . . ."

"On his life," Alice finished for her.

"Cordell has plenty of money," James reasoned. "Let him hire a guard."

"Like in the movies?" Alice's eyes widened, but James was serious.

"If I was in his shoes and had his wealth, you'd better believe I'd be playing it cautious," he said.

"Maybe Maggie's all wet," Trent said. "Maybe Perkins isn't responsible."

"Who else could it be?" Alice reasoned. "Perkins had no business at the nurses' station. Oh, he drops by once in a while for a word with his mother. But he had no excuse for picking up a chart. They are strictly confidential. That's the rule, and Nadine, Perkins's mother, is a stickler for rules."

"Maybe it was his doctor," Justin injected, tiring of the matter.

"Or a nurse," Trent said.

"Or his girlfriend, Miss Fontana," was Justin's second guess. He grinned broadly. "Never trust a good-looking dame. Especially when she's your beneficiary."

"Where'd you hear that?" Trent goaded him. "Been reading the social page lately?"

Alice was drawn into their lighthearted guessing game, but Maggie sat silently by. Cole Cordell was more than an interesting topic for dinner conversation.

Later, as Alice helped with the dishes, she commented, "You know, Maggie, you're lucky. Being an only child is highly overrated, take it from me."

"Brothers have their moments," Maggie admitted. "They can also be a trial."

Alice took a plate from the drain and dried it. "Still, you never lack for company. My apartment gets lonely sometimes." She turned an anxious face on Maggie. "You don't mind my dropping in like this, do you?"

"Goodness no. I enjoy your company. And so do the boys."

Alice's mouth drooped. "Justin and

Trent, perhaps. But I fear Jim finds me a nuisance."

Maggie patted her arm and encouraged, "James is warming some. Frankly, his reaction the other night was partly my fault. He thought I was playing matchmaker and that made him leery."

"Does he hate women in general or just me?"

Maggie laughed at the woebegone expression in her friend's blue eyes. "James doesn't hate you. He's just slow to warm up to anyone." Folding the dish cloth over the middle of the double sink, she added, "He's a bit hard to understand. Since our parents' death, he's made raising me and running the farm his dual goal in life. And he doesn't adjust to changes very well."

"So I noticed," Alice remarked. "He positively glowers whenever you talk about your work at the hospital."

Maggie sighed. "He still considers me his responsibility. And he finds independence in me — even in the boys — hard to stomach."

"Don't rock the boat?"

Maggie agreed that was her eldest brother's attitude. "He likes the way we've stayed together through thick and thin and kept the farm afloat. And he fears if we start pulling in different directions, it'll all come tumbling down around us."

Alice sniffed her disapproval. "He sounds like a positive dictator. I can't imagine why I'm the least bit attracted to him."

Laughing at her frank admission, Maggie commented, "Maybe it's true about opposites attracting. A good shaking up is what James needs. Maybe you're just the girl to give it to him."

"Me?" Alice asked. "How could I shake him up? He considers me totally incompetent. He never heard of anyone being afraid of cows."

Maggie yelped, "You told him that?"

"Well, what was I supposed to do?" Alice demanded. "Justin and Trent were determined I was going to the barn with them while they milked. In the interest of self-preservation, I finally admitted I was scared of cows."

Maggie tried to smother her giggles and nearly choked instead. "What did James say?" she managed to ask.

"Not much. But he looked as if he thought I'd dropped down from another planet," she confessed miserably.

"Yes, sir, Alice, you could be the best thing ever to happen to James," Maggie repeated with growing conviction.

"James!" Alice sighed. "It sounds so formal. No wonder he's so starchy. I prefer Jim myself."

With that, her self-confidence returned. She tossed Maggie her towel and marched into the living room. "Justin? Trent? Jim? How about a game of bridge?"

Bridge? Maggie went into gales of laughter. The only bridge James was familiar with was the bridge that passed over a body of water.

Yet give Alice credit, she got the three of them gathered around the kitchen table, produced a deck of cards from her pocketbook, and, with Maggie looking on, began explaining the game.

CHAPTER SEVEN

Intending to take James's advice about informing Cole of her suspicions in regard to Wade Perkins, Maggie arose early on Sunday morning and arrived a full thirty minutes before her shift began.

To her surprise, a uniformed guard stood at the door of Cole's room. Flustered, Maggie changed direction and returned to the nurses' station.

"What gives with Cole Cordell?" she asked the nurse on duty.

The nurse looked up from her paper work. "The hospital staff has determined he needs protection, so they're providing it." The woman dismissed Maggie, bending her head down to the work before her.

Uncertain whether or not she'd be allowed to see Cole, Maggie approached the guard. "Hi," she greeted him a bit timidly. "May I go in?"

The guard studied her light-blue uniform with sleepy eyes. "You work here?" he asked.

Maggie nodded and explained. "I don't go on duty until seven. I came in early to have a word with Mr. Cordell. May I?"

Shrugging, the guard allowed her to pass. Some guard, she thought not too impressed with how easily he'd allowed her to gain admittance.

Her hand found the wall switch and the bright light flooded the room. Cole blinked against the glare. He ran a hand through his dark hair.

Reaching for the lever to bring the upper portion of the bed to a sitting position, he asked, "How'd you get past the clown?"

"It wasn't even a challenge."

"I told them I didn't need him, didn't even want him," Cole grumbled. "But I guess they're probably protecting themselves as much as they are me. Kirsten's threat of a lawsuit has Mr. Dempster in a cold sweat."

"Truthfully, I found the guard a disappointment. He didn't even ask my name, much less to see any identification." Smiling, she went to Cole's bedside.

"With those innocent green eyes, you appear harmless enough." Cole himself eased into a more comfortable position and rubbed a stubbly chin. "What brings you in so early?"

"I wanted a chance to talk to you." Maggie pulled a chair up to his bed and, wondering where to begin, perched on the edge of it.

Cole's gaze, as it ran over her, was enlivened by a spark of mischief. "If this is a heart-to-heart confession of undying love, let me shave and make myself more presentable."

"No, nothing like that." Tamping down flustered feelings, Maggie plunged into how she'd come to suspect Wade Perkins was responsible for the changes on Cole's chart. Her gaze on Cole's face, she fell silent, leaving him to mull it over.

"I see what you're saying," he said when the silence had lengthened. "And I admit your theory could be correct — Perkins does hate me. But . . ."

He trailed off, frowning as he tried to puzzle it out. "The guard at my door is compliments of the hospital because, in going over my chart, they discovered the allergy notation wasn't the only thing which had been altered.

"A lot of misinformation was scattered throughout the chart, misinformation that — given the right set of circumstances — could have buried me."

Maggie gasped. "So they've decided someone was definitely trying to kill you!"

"Thus the posted guard," he finished.

"I still don't see why you doubt but that it was Perkins."

"There's one simple hitch. Do you realize how time-consuming it must have been to make the number of changes which had been made?" he reasoned. "How much time would you say Perkins had with that chart on the day you saw him, assuming it was my chart?"

"No more than five minutes," Maggie replied. "Maybe less."

"Then you see how unlikely it is that he would have had sufficient time."

Reluctantly, Maggie conceded his point. Then, on second thought, she said, "Suppose he didn't do it all at one time? Suppose he got his hands on that chart another time, a more lengthy time! Or suppose he switched charts!"

With his doubtful expression cast upon her, Maggie rose from her chair to insist, "It could be, Cole. You said yourself you thought Wade Perkins came to your room following your surgery. But at the time you were still groggy and later decided you must have imagined it."

Still skeptical, Cole swung out of bed and reached for his robe. Moving stiffly toward the window which overlooked the employees' parking lot, he granted, "Maybe

I didn't imagine it after all. Even then it doesn't prove he messed with my chart. I wish I could recall it more clearly. It was so fuzzy in my mind, that's why I assumed it was a dream."

Excitement mounting, Maggie joined him at the window. "Maybe someone else saw him that day." She paused a moment to consider. "Do you remember if he spoke to you? Or," she remedied, "if you imagined that he spoke to you that day?"

"The snatch I recall isn't fit for a lady's ears," he said dryly.

"He threatened you?" Maggie pressed.

"Not threatened exactly." He looked away from her and muttered, "But he made more ugly accusations about Rhoda and me."

"Rhoda?" The intonation of his voice set off a bell in her mind. She'd heard Cole speak of Rhoda before.

"Wade's wife," he said. "We grew up together. And through the years, our paths have crossed a few times."

"And Wade Perkins thinks you . . ." Maggie caught herself in mid-sentence and wished she could bow out of this conversation. She had a reluctance to hear about Wade Perkins's estranged wife.

Cole said, "Perkins was raving about the

visit Rhoda had paid me early the morning of my surgery."

"She did come visit you? Or Perkins just thought she did?" Maggie sought to get it straight in her mind.

"She came in very early and talked awhile. As I said, we grew up good friends."

There was no reason his evasive gazing out the window while he was on the subject of Rhoda should cause her such pain. She had no claim on him. It was getting to be a long line, anyway. Kirsten. Rhoda. Who else lurked in the wings? she wondered, watching cars flow into the parking lot outside. This definitely was not a man to trust where the ladies were concerned.

So why did her heartbeat quicken when he drew a step nearer? Why did she tremble when he tipped her chin up and, with that mischievous glint in his gray eyes, say, "Jealous?"

"Who me?" She fought for composure. "You must be joking!" The warmth of his thumb caressing her chin evoked a flood of disturbing feelings. "You're only in need of a little tender, loving care for another day or two. Then, like Mr. Jenkins down the hall, you'll be gone and soon forgotten."

His smile bordered on amused tolerance. Tracing the delicate curve of her jawbone up to her ear, he said, "You know better, Maggie."

Maggie jerked away from him. A telltale quiver disturbing her voice, she accused, "You're nothing but a smooth talker and a handsome face, Mr. Cordell. No different from Mr. Jenkins."

He laughed mockingly. "About fifty years different, I'd say. I've met your Mr. Jenkins. He and I exchanged a few words yesterday as he was preparing to leave. Hey!" he objected as she darted toward the door. "Where are you going?"

"I need a cup of coffee before I clock in," she claimed when in truth it was Nadine's car pulling into the lot which had set her feet to scurrying. Recalling the original purpose of her visit, Maggie paused long enough to ask, "Do you want me to relay to Mr. Dempster that I saw Wade Perkins fooling with a chart prior to your penicillin mix-up?"

"No need in your taking the heat," he said without pause. "Under the circumstances, I doubt it would endear you to Nadine Perkins. I'd noticed you are a little timid where she's concerned." There was a pause.

Cole finally added, "I'll enlighten Mr. Dempster and keep your name out of the process. I'm not all that convinced it was

98

Perkins anyhow. He has a big mouth, but he's a gutless wimp."

Satisfied to let it rest with him, Maggie hurried out of Cole's room. The guard had come by a chair and sat slouched in it, his cap all but covering his sleepy eyes.

"How's the patient?" he roused himself to ask.

"Fine," Maggie murmured. Pausing, she offered, "I'm going for a roll and coffee. Could I bring something back for you?"

Little knowing she offered in the hopes black coffee would make him more attentive, the guard accepted.

The coffee shop was all but empty, since most of the hospital employees chose the cafeteria for its more social atmosphere. Maggie wanted to be alone, away from the maddening chatter of people who appeared not to have a care in the world. This business with Cole was going from bad to worse.

He might take it casually, but the fact was, someone was out to see him leave Bartlett's Medical Complex in an undertaker's car!

How could he remain so calm about the whole thing? she wondered. But then, perhaps his serene attitude was part of his attraction, she mused, slipping into yet another level of worry.

Though it was terrifying to admit, somewhere along the line she'd moved past a dreamy-eyed schoolgirl infatuation. Her feelings for Cole Cordell ran deep and mysterious. The sometimes glorious, sometimes painful, blush of womanhood was mingled with a fear of having her love returned in like measure. Sure, he flirted with her. His eyes were warm as they beheld her. And his lips curved in an affectionate smile. Yet he was generations ahead of her in this grown-up world of love. Still, her love defied all the warning messages her brain beamed to her foolish heart.

Maggie drank down her last swallow of coffee and beckoned for the waitress. As she did, Nadine Perkins spotted her from the doorway.

Clear-cut purpose marking each determined step, she came toward Maggie. Without allowing a hello, she spoke tersely. "Sit down again, Maggie. I want a word with you."

Filled with misgivings, Maggie did as she was told.

"I guess you know that was my son, Wade, with me last evening," she began, then broke off again when the waitress came to their table.

Maggie gave the girl the guard's order. Then Nadine waved her away. Tapping an impatient foot, she began again.

"About Wade. He told me where he'd run into you before."

"Oh?"

"Let's not mince words, Maggie," Nadine said, her mouth a thin, ominous line. "I'm aware you're sharp-eyed and not at all slow to put two and two together. However, in this case, my fear is you'll come up with the wrong answer." She paused, yet when Maggie remained silent, seemed unsettled. "Would you care to divulge any conclusions you've drawn?" she snapped.

"Nadine . . ." Maggie hesitated, then continued with difficulty. "It isn't my place to draw conclusions."

"Exactly!" Nadine said.

"But," Maggie continued in a small voice, "I can't ignore what I saw. Your son had a patient chart in his hands that day I ran into him at the nurses' station. And he purposely sent me away."

"It wasn't Cole Cordell's chart," Nadine stated, not quite meeting Maggie's eyes. "I know because I came upon him only moments after you'd gone to Mr. Jenkins's room."

"Whose chart was it?"

"That isn't important," Nadine said. "Admittedly Wade had no business

101

touching any of the charts. But he is fidgety by nature. He wasn't looking at the chart. He was merely passing time while he waited for a word with me."

"Nadine —"

Nadine cut her short. "No, listen to me! If it had been something else lying there, he would have picked it up instead. Or doodled on the phone directory. Or restacked a pile of papers. It's nervous energy. He didn't pick Cole's chart up to tamper with it."

"So it *was* Cole's chart!"

"Purely coincidental!" Nadine insisted, clearly miffed she'd given that away. Ever icy blue eyes swept over Maggie. "I pride myself on being a good nurse, on not letting my personal feelings enter in. But there is one thing that comes before my nursing. That is Wade. I'm warning you, don't make waves about this."

Though Maggie uttered not a word, she could not help the light of rebellion in her eyes. Nadine tried to quench it with a threat.

"I've worked in this hospital for twenty years, Maggie. No one is going to take your word over mine. You'd do best to remember that. For if I catch so much as a whisper of Wade's name in connection with the Cole Cordell matter, you're out the door. If I can't find a reason to fire you, I'll invent one. Do you understand me?"

Without awaiting her reply Nadine stamped out. Maggie waited until she was out of view to trust her body weight to wobbly legs. Taking the coffee and roll in hands that trembled, she drew a steadying breath and made her exit.

On duty, Nadine spoke to Maggie as if her ominous warning in the coffee shop had never taken place. Maggie was so unnerved by the whole ordeal, it seemed her hands would not perform her regular chores with yesterday's efficiency.

Sheets refused to go on hospital beds without a ripple. She slopped a cup of warm tea down the quilted robe of a gentle elderly patient who needed assistance with breakfast. And another woman patient complained she'd nearly rubbed the hide off her, administering a back massage.

Maggie was about at her wits' end. She didn't like the woman's superior attitude in the first place. And in the second place, she didn't think the woman even needed the rubdown. She'd had a couple of moles removed, for crying out loud!

Yet Maggie apologized profusely, then proceeded to apply bath powder to the woman. Haughtily, the woman asked that she leave before she caused her to sneeze away all the benefits of her "difficult cosmetic surgery."

Difficult cosmetic surgery. Maggie snickered to herself. She'd never seen anyone make such an ordeal out of a couple of moles. The woman should have been released two days ago! Maggie couldn't understand why she was still around. Unless there were complications she didn't know of.

Nadine did not appear to notice her avoidance of Cole's room. What would her reaction have been, Maggie wondered, if she'd known Maggie was steering clear of him for fear he'd wrangle the episode with Nadine out of her and subsequently refuse to tell Mr. Dempster about Wade Perkins? She very well might get fired when word reached Nadine's ears, despite the fact Maggie wouldn't be the one to inform on Wade. Not directly anyway. Come what may, Maggie wasn't going to ask Cole to keep quiet for her job's sake.

For what was her job, weighed against Cole's life? With that thought in mind, Maggie endured a morning fraught with anxieties and bid her lunch hour a grateful hello.

Finding the usual din of the cafeteria jarring to her nerves, Maggie went through the line, then carried her tray to the outer courtyard. The sun was warm on the concrete table, but the October breeze was chilly. Maggie likened the contrast to the hot/cold dry ice feeling in the pit of her stomach. With difficulty, she held fears and dread at bay and picked up her sandwich.

"Hey, Maggie! I wondered where you disappeared to," Alice called from the sliding glass door. "Aren't you cold out here? Come inside and eat with me."

"I'm not cold," Maggie murmured and kept her seat.

A frown puckered Alice's brow. "What's wrong?" she asked. When Maggie made no reply, she disappeared a moment, then reappeared with her own tray.

"May as well freeze along with you," she said cheerily and sent Maggie a quick sidelong glance. "You've been on edge all morning. Care to confide in me?"

"I'm just having a bad day, that's all," Maggie hedged.

Alice's freckled face creased into a smile. "You aren't the only one. If misery loves company, then join Nadine's ranks. She's been a bear all morning!"

Maggie's hand stiffened as she reached for her Coke. She fumbled with the straw and accidentally tipped her glass on top of her sandwich. She exclaimed, "This is how my whole morning has gone! Can you believe it? I spilled a cup of tea in sweet Miss Meeker's lap, spilled powder all over that snobby Mrs. Rollsroyce, and —"

"Mrs. Rollsroyce?" Alice leaned on the table and laughed. "Where'd you pick that up?"

"I can never remember her name," Maggie complained. "Rolls something-or-the-other. What it amounts to is she's rolling in money and wants to make certain we all stoop and bow. Difficult cosmetic surgery," Maggie muttered disagreeably. "The woman had a couple of moles removed. You'd think she had a major operation the way she talks. And she's been here long enough to have had her bottom lifted too! What gives with her anyway?"

"It's all very hush-hush," Alice confided, lowering her voice. "But they're running some tests, fearing a tumor of the brain."

Experiencing a pang of guilt that she'd been so ungracious about the woman, Maggie amended, "Then maybe she has an excuse for her bad manners. I'm sorry I talked about her."

"Don't be." Alice chuckled. "She's probably been obnoxious all her life anyway."

Shoving her plate toward Maggie, she added, "Take half my sandwich. I don't need it anyway."

At her insistence, Maggie took it. Swallowing became a difficult matter a moment later when Alice blithely informed her, "Rumors are flying hot and heavy about Wade Perkins. It'd be my guess that's what has put the fine-honed edge to Nadine's tongue."

A shiver ran through Maggie. "Rumors?"

"You know. About the Cole Cordell thing," Alice went on. "It's going through the corridor like forest fire. I do feel kind of sorry for Nadine. I mean, she isn't responsible for Wade's crazy behavior, is she?"

"No. But she's responsible for her own!" Maggie burst out. Then beneath Alice's concerned countenance, the whole story of Nadine's threat tumbled out.

Wide-eyed and disbelieving, Alice gawked at Maggie. "Are we talking about the same Nadine Perkins? The Nadine who has worked here for twenty-odd years without a single blemish on her record? Maggie, you must have misunderstood."

"If I misunderstood, then there is a slim chance I may still have my job this time tomorrow. But I wouldn't lay odds on it, Alice. She said it, and she meant every word." Trying to mop up the remains of her Coke with a napkin, Maggie added, "And it looks to me like Nadine could see what a mistake she's making. She can't cover up for her son. Before it's all said and done, he'll drag her down with him."

"Unless she's right and Wade is innocent."

"Oh, come on, Alice," Maggie said impatiently. "You surely don't believe that."

"Not totally. But somehow I can't feature Nadine so determinedly defending Wade unless she really believed he was innocent, but in danger of being thought guilty."

"You know her better than I do," Maggie said, unwilling to argue with Alice. "My main point is, if it wasn't Wade, then who? Who else would have the motivation to take such a risk? It's common knowledge Wade hates Cole."

"I know it's unlikely, but there is still Kirsten," Alice pointed out.

"Kirsten? She's engaged to him . . . or whatever," Maggie finished lamely, for she wasn't too clear on that either.

"Still, who has more to gain than she by Cordell's death?" Alice reasoned. She twirled her straw. "Your brother wasn't kidding. She really is his beneficiary, for the most part. Kirsten's mother, who is rumored to be somewhere in the Orient, was granted a lifelong allowance by the late Coleman Cordell's will. So she'd have nothing to gain by young Cole's death."

"Where do you get all your information?" Maggie asked.

Alice grinned cheekily. "I keep my ears to the ground."

Pushing her messy tray aside, Maggie confided, "Kirsten Fontana isn't the only woman in Cole's life. Did you know Wade's wife had been in to visit Cole the morning before his surgery?"

Alice laughed at her. "You sound as Victorian as your brother, Jim. Rhoda and Cole grew up together. I don't find her visiting him in the hospital unusual."

"Apparently Wade did," Maggie murmured. "He paid Cole a visit and had a few unpleasant things to say about his wife's visit."

Alice's eyes lit up with interest. "You mentioned that last evening. But did you ever determine whether Wade did really visit Cole? You said he may have just dreamed it."

"Cole was vague on it," Maggie admitted. "I guess there's a possibility it was just a dream."

Having finished her meal, Alice pulled

her sweater closer. "Brr. It feels awfully cold out here to me. Let's go back inside."

Maggie hung back a moment longer. "Have you met this Rhoda? I mean, do you know her personally?"

"Sure," Alice replied. "Rhoda worked here at Bartlett's three or four years ago. She was a pretty good nurse. It was Nadine who introduced her to Wade."

"How in the world did Wade ever steal her away from Cole Cordell?" Maggie wondered aloud.

Alice chuckled. "I know you're quite blind to anyone but Cole, but the fact is, Wade Perkins isn't a bad-looking man either. Maybe he simply swept Rhoda off her feet. Or maybe Cole was willing to have her stolen away — maybe he'd tired of her. I don't really know."

Alice took her tray through the sliding glass door. As they made their way through the cafeteria, she changed the subject.

"Would I appear awfully pushy if I were to drop by your house again tonight? I do believe Jim is beginning to warm up to me."

"It's definitely James? Not Justin or Trent?" Maggie asked, eager to share Alice's confidences where her brothers were concerned.

Alice's eyes flickered in self-mockery. "I never could resist a challenge."

"James'll be that, for sure," Maggie assured her. "In the first place, Justin and Trent have staked a prior interest. He won't climb over them to get to you."

"Sure, he will." Alice chuckled. "All's fair in love and war. Where've you been, Maggie?"

"I hate to shoot holes in your confidence, but what *are* you going to do about Justin and Trent?"

"I'm handling that matter," Alice assured her as they approached the surgical ward. "You know that stunning blonde in radiology? The one with the violet eyes? I'm going to arrange a blind date for her with Trent."

"Never," Maggie said, shaking her head. "Trent's too shy for a blind date."

"Really?" Alice blew out a sigh and reconsidered. "Then maybe Justin."

"You do stand a better chance with Justin. He likes tall blondes." She hastened to keep up with Alice. "But there is still the problem of Trent."

"I'm satisfied to climb one mountain at a time." Alice gave a careless shrug. "I'll work something out. But by hook or by crook, I'm going to get Jim to take me seriously. Wait and see!"

Alice sidestepped a wheelchair, turned, and gave Maggie a cocky grin. "Just wait and see."

CHAPTER EIGHT

Contrary to her word, Alice did not drive out to the farm that evening. Maggie washed up the supper dishes and wondered what had kept her away. Maybe she had some sly notion she'd be more noticeable by her absence.

And maybe she had a point.

Over supper Trent had asked, "Is Alice coming out to play bridge again?"

"She mentioned she might," Maggie had replied, noting that none of her brothers seemed displeased at the prospect.

However, as the evening had lengthened and Alice had not arrived, their spirits had dropped.

Trent and Justin dozed through a television show and James wandered out to the barn, having claimed he had work to do.

All in all, it was an uninspiring evening. Maggie spent it wondering if she had a job to return to in the morning. That the phone did not ring all evening seemed a good omen. Perhaps Nadine had reconsidered and had not acted upon her threat.

Thus cheered, it was with sky-diving

spirits that Maggie was greeted the next morning by a glacier-eyed, grim-lipped Nadine. The firing came like sudden death. Words like "insubordinate," "irresponsible," "unreliable," and "short-tempered" pierced Maggie like needles.

Taking it to a higher court seemed a futile effort. So full of the dread of facing James with the news, Maggie drove home. The house was a welcoming haven of serenity in a stormy world. James, Justin, and Trent, busy with the harvest, weren't likely to make an appearance before noon. That, at least, gave her time to ready her explanation.

Maggie sat at the kitchen table, nursing a cup of hot cocoa. She'd never known her pride could take such a battering! Maybe she should have gone to Mr. Dempster and told him the true story, suggesting he talk to her fellow workers and some of the patients.

With her luck, she mused sourly, he'd have chosen Mrs. Rollsroyce. Some help that would have been! That woman had taken an instinctive dislike to her.

Furthermore, it was common knowledge Nadine and Mr. Dempster were thicker than thieves. Talking with him would not have given her her job back. His loyalty would have been to Nadine and her twenty-odd years of faultless service.

No. Far better to take it on the chin. The phone rang, making her nerves jump. Maggie sloshed cocoa into the saucer as she pushed away from the table and went to the phone.

"Maggie?" Cole asked.

Her heart leaping at the sound of his smooth, low voice, Maggie responded in the affirmative.

"You haven't drowned in a pool of self-pity?" he teased her gently.

"So you heard." She expelled a weary sigh. "I've managed to stay afloat."

"Too bad. I was going to offer to resuscitate you. Mouth to mouth," he added. "It'd be my pleasure."

Maggie forced a lightness of spirit she did not feel. "Flattery always cheers a girl."

"Seriously, I called to say I'm sorry you lost your job. I feel responsible."

"No need for you to."

"Your friend, Alice, was in. She told me Nadine Perkins had threatened to fire you if you didn't keep quiet about Wade."

Maggie sighed. "Turns out, it wasn't a threat."

"I really am sorry, Maggie," he apologized again. "And if you think it would do any good, I'll have a talk with Dempster and explain the situation. I'm certain he has the authority to intervene."

Maggie was touched that he should offer. But there was such a thing as pride. "Thanks, but no thanks," she murmured. "Working under Nadine after all that has happened would be impossible. I wouldn't come back if they begged me to."

"Not even to pick me up?" he questioned. "You did say you would if need be."

"Don't ask me to," Maggie pleaded. "I lack what it takes to face all the curious whispering eyes."

"No, you don't. Just stick out that cute chin of yours and mow them down with a green-eyed stare." He chuckled softly. "They wouldn't dare risk asking a single question. Say you'll come get me, Maggie."

"In other words, you didn't get a driver and Kirsten's still mad," Maggie guessed.

"Kirsten is still giving me the cold shoulder, yes," he admitted. "And as for the driver, I got one call about the ad."

"And?"

"And in checking him out, I discovered his license had been suspended three months ago. Reckless driving."

"Your luck is running on par with mine, it would seem," Maggie sympathized.

"I'm not too disheartened. I'd rather have a certain pretty girl with a freckle on her lip drive me anyway," he said, his tone low and husky.

"Cole —"

"The doctor is coming in about nine," he interrupted. "So I'd guess I'll be ready to go about ten-thirty or eleven. I'll treat you to lunch." Giving her no time for further argument, he hung up the phone.

Maggie considered phoning him back, telling him to find someone else. Surely in his position he could have summoned one of a dozen people to come pick him up from the hospital.

Yet he'd asked her. Despite how hard she tried not to be, Maggie was flattered. Flattered enough to ignore the unpleasant sensation the idea of walking back onto the surgical recovery ward gave her.

She wiled the morning away catching up on housework, then dressed in warm slacks and a sweater of hunter green. Modestly aware the outfit emphasized the green of her eyes in a most flattering way, Maggie hummed a nervous tune as she drove back to Bartlett's.

Once inside the door, Maggie drew a steadying breath, took the corridor down to the surgical ward and faced Nadine's frosty-eyed glower without exchanging a word.

The guard at Cole's door gave her a nod

117

of recognition and she went right in. Cole was dressed and waiting.

Greeting her with a crooked smile, he admitted, "I wasn't sure you'd show."

Not wishing to linger any longer than necessary, Maggie asked, "Are you ready to go?"

He was, and at his summons a practical nurse appeared, exchanged an ill-at-ease greeting with Maggie, then produced a wheelchair for Cole. Carrying his suitcase, Maggie followed his exit parade down the corridor and out the wide doors to her car.

When Cole was settled in the passenger's seat and the nurse had gone, he turned to her with an upbeat grin. "See? That wasn't so bad, now was it?"

Exasperated by his cheerfulness, Maggie made a face at him. "Easy for *you* to say. If looks could kill, Nadine would have slain me at first glance."

"What'd she have to say?" he asked as Maggie put the car into motion.

"I didn't give her the chance to say anything," she admitted, then quickly changed the subject as she steered the car down the main street of the town of Bartlett. "How does it feel to leave your shadow behind?"

"The guard?" Cole laughed. "I can't say I miss him. He wasn't much fun. I tried to get

118

him to play cards with me last evening, but he claimed he was on duty."

"Sleeping duty, no doubt," Maggie returned dryly.

"No, this wasn't the same fellow. This character was very diligent. Made half the nurses show their identification before letting them pass."

"What were half the nurses doing in your room?" Maggie was quick to ask.

Lines of amusement framing his mouth, Cole remarked, "And here I was beginning to think you didn't care."

Uncomfortably aware of his teasing gaze, Maggie said, "You misunderstand. What I mean was, was there more trouble? What brought half the nurses to your room?"

"No, no more trouble. They were just being diligent in their care. That's the password at Bartlett's these days — diligent. Mr. Dempster still worries I might sue."

Realizing his mention of nurses had been an exaggeration intended to get a rise out of her, Maggie kept quiet. Not until she reached the four-way stop that led onto the highway to Madison did she speak again.

"You're going to have to give me directions to your house. Do I take the highway?"

"It's the closest way," Cole replied. "But in view of those potholes, I've a better idea."

"Which is?" Maggie braked to a stop.

"Let's pull into that hamburger stand, get lunch to go, and take the scenic route home."

"Won't the country roads be as rough as the highway?"

Cole shrugged off her concern. "We can take it slow. We're in no hurry, are we?" When Maggie admitted she had no plans for the afternoon, he added, "Then let's enjoy the day. It's Indian summer weather. We may as well make the most of it."

His spur-of-the-moment plans agreeable to her, Maggie pulled into the roadside restaurant, then, moments later, pulled out again with a sack of food between them on the seat.

"Do we eat along the way?" she asked.

Cole shook a sorrowful head. "Where's your sense of romance? Find a scenic overlook and pull over to eat. Take the road to the east here."

It was a blacktop road and fairly smooth. Still, Maggie kept to a leisurely speed. As Cole had observed, it was a beautiful autumn day. Huge combines chewed away at golden fields of corn. They seemed a space-age contradiction to nearby rusted windmills, leaning fence posts, and outbuildings gray and abused by time.

But the farmers driving the huge machinery returned a friendly wave as they harvested their ripe fields and Maggie found her spirits lifting. Some things never changed, rural friendliness being one example.

As they crested a steep hill, Cole pointed out an overgrown drive, suggesting she pull in. Maggie did so. There was something nostalgic about the tumbledown, long-abandoned old farmhouse.

They unwrapped sandwiches and began to eat in a companionable silence. Maggie gazed out the car window. Waving weeds encroached upon the sagging stone foundation of the paint-peeled old farmhouse. A lone squirrel dashing up the side of the house was the only sign of life.

Preoccupied with her own thoughts, she sighed a wistful sigh and sipped her soft drink.

"What's the matter?" Cole asked. He slid her a questioning glance.

"Does it ever strike you how transitory life is?" Maggie asked, her gaze drifting all around her. "How this tumble-down farm holds the story of people who lived and worked hard to get by, how they laughed and loved and . . ."

"Died?" Cole questioned. Humoring her,

he pointed down the hillside. "Maybe these particular folks haven't gone the full route. I'll bet they built that new ranch house down there. So see? You don't have to look so sad."

"But they abandoned the old house. It stands empty and useless. I think that's sad."

"The roof probably leaked," he said on a note of practicality. "Cold winter winds blew through the place as if the walls were paper. And I'll bet the plumbing was bad."

Maggie shook a finger at him. "And you accused me of lacking romanticism."

He grinned. "It's tough getting romantic about old houses. Now a pretty girl . . ." He pulled a curl that lay soft against her neck. Eyes full of devilment, he said, "Finish eating and we'll talk more about that later."

And true to his word, he did, though it was slow in coming. They'd finished the last scrap of food when Cole swung his car door open, saying, "Let's get out a minute. I need some fresh air."

"Don't you think you should get home where you can rest?" Maggie asked.

A slight frown running between his dark brows, he remarked, "I hope you're not going to be a conscientious little killjoy."

Sensitive beyond reason to his bantering

criticism, Maggie reached for the door handle. "I guess you know your limitations. Did you have some strenuous hill-climbing in mind? Or shall we just jog a mile or two?"

His mouth twisted into another grin. "You've made your point. Just prop me against the car, Nurse Maggie. I'll breathe some country air, enjoy the autumn scenery a moment, then, like the docile fellow I am, I'll allow you to drive me straight home."

"Prop yourself," Maggie retorted. She climbed out and walked to the front of her car. He joined her, draped an arm around her shoulder, and, leaning on her heavily, teased, "All right, I will."

Jangled nerves scattering in all directions, Maggie disentangled herself, saying pointedly, "Against the car, not me."

"You really are a killjoy!" His eyes held a hint of mockery in their gray depths.

Cut to the quick, Maggie moved away from him. "It really is Indian summer. Cobwebs, the scent of burning leaves." Her words tumbled out in nervous haste. She talked on, pointing down the hillside where fields were measured off like patchwork quilts, some of uncut grain, some of corn stubble, some plowed ground. In a distant field a combine ground to a halt. The operator, miniature in size from their vantage point, climbed down and stooped to examine something.

"Should have bought a Cordell harvester," Maggie said lightly and turned, expecting to win a smile from Cole.

But his expression as he contemplated her was dark and hidden.

A fluttery sensation disrupted Maggie's breathing. "What is it?" she asked.

"I was wondering why you shy away so easily," he said. "Would it sound overconfident if I were to say I've noted you view me with a certain interest?"

Rueing the color that flagged her cheeks, Maggie protested, "I hardly know you."

"I'm doing my best to alter that. You might cooperate." He advanced at an unhurried pace. Dark lashes flicked down, then up, to reveal eyes sparked with humor. He tipped up her chin. "Mightn't you?"

"For what purpose?" she demanded. "I'd think two women jumping attendance on you would be plenty."

He asked, "Two?"

Quivering inside, Maggie retorted, "Yes, two! Miss Fontana, your fiancee. Remember her? And Rhoda Perkins. I would say, in visiting you, she went beyond the call of duty for an old sweetheart."

"You *are* jealous. I adore a jealous

woman," he teased and, without warning, deposited a light kiss on her protesting mouth.

Washed in confusion, Maggie stammered, "I'm not a trifler, Cole."

Laughter darkened his eyes. "Who's trifling?"

His arms found their way around her, his mouth covered her words, and, refusing to release her, he kissed her more thoroughly. His demanding lips set off an explosion of ecstasy, like sunshine, sweet clover, and the warm touch of velvet. Yet Maggie fought the good feeling, fought him too until he had no choice but to let her go.

Heart thundering, voice quivering, she said, "If you want a ride home, you'd best get in. I've half a mind to leave you." She sped to her side of the car and yanked the door open.

"Stranded?" he said. "You're much too conscientious to leave an injured man stranded."

"Don't bet on it," Maggie retorted threateningly and slammed her door hard.

He slid in beside her and closed his own door more quietly. He said nothing until they were rolling along the road again. Then, tossing her a sideways glance, he informed her, "Six days ago, you wouldn't have eluded me so easily."

"Arrogance does not become you, Cole Cordell," Maggie informed him, her voice trembling with emotion.

He seemed surprised she'd taken his comment as a brag. "I'm only being honest, Maggie. You're as aware of the sparks as I am."

Maggie found his frankness most disconcerting. She stared straight ahead at the gently rolling countryside, refusing to spare him so much as a glance.

"If I hadn't scored so many bad marks with what you seem to consider a disturbing number of lady friends, I'd have won you over in a minute." Though his tone was bantering, Maggie suspected he was serious.

"And if the well hadn't gone dry, the cows wouldn't have died of thirst!" she muttered.

"If it would alter matters between us, I can make you understand about Rhoda, though I'm reluctant to do so. As for Kirsten, she's a little more difficult to explain. Sometimes I'm not sure I understand myself," he confessed.

Maggie tried to wither him with a look. "Spare me all the sordid details."

It seemed he was a hard man to discourage. Despite her unfriendly countenance, he was cheerful with the directions he gave at each crossroad. And when numerous attempts at conversation failed to rouse her from her moody silence, he too became quiet. But it was a quiet broken by an occasional private chuckle.

CHAPTER NINE

Maggie was ill-prepared for the simple grandeur of Cole's country estate. Iron gates stood open to reveal a tree-scattered lawn, a lawn which had felt the first strokes of Jack Frost's brush, lawn colorfully arrayed in golds and browns and reds.

There was nothing trendy about the solid two-story white house which stood like a fortress up the long, winding lane. Majestic columns supported the veranda roof, which did double duty as an upper balcony.

Hardy autumn flowers created a splash of plum and gold and white. With a crunch of white rock, Maggie slowed the car to a stop on the horseshoe-shaped drive.

Startled out of her silence, she exclaimed, "You live here all by yourself? This place is huge!"

A look of modest pleasure spread across his face. "No, not alone. Bart Davis, my jack-of-all-trades handyman, lives in the rooms over the garage." Cole pointed to a low-slung building a discreet distance away. "And I have a live-in housekeeper. My father had the house built about twenty years ago. Do you like it?"

"It's lovely," Maggie exclaimed. "But I would have guessed it to be much older."

"It was built with that intention," Cole told her. "Dad had reached an age where the past seemed more fashionable than the present. He was born and raised in the South and he brought to the house a flavor of Colonial America mixed in with the grace of an old Southern mansion. At least, that was his purpose."

"He achieved it admirably." Making no attempt to climb out of the car, Maggie gazed at the house a moment longer.

Cole stirred in the seat. "Shall we go in?"

Belatedly realizing she was staring like a star-struck tourist, Maggie scrambled out of the car. Taking Cole's suitcase from the back seat, she followed him up a wide brick walkway.

Cole held the door for her. "Go right in. Birdie, my housekeeper, is a little hard of hearing. Just leave the suitcase in the foyer. She'll get it later."

Her mission of bringing him home accomplished, Maggie knew she should go. Yet when Cole took her arm and ushered her into the spacious front room, curiosity stole away her better judgment.

Spotting the spiral staircase, Maggie stifled an outcry of delight. "It wouldn't surprise me to see Scarlett O'Hara come floating down in an elegant gown," she said, and Cole squeezed her arm.

"My father would be pleased." He stayed at her side, seeming to draw pleasure from her reaction to the huge, high-ceilinged room.

A small fire crackled on the generous hearth of the stone fireplace. Maggie counted not one, but three couches, excellent reproductions of a bygone era.

A spinet piano occupied a corner. Wide windows facing the front of the house were framed by luxurious drapes and sweeping valances of a rose print.

A deeper shade of rose was woven into the design of the Oriental carpet beneath her feet. At the far end of the room, French doors led out to a screened-in porch. Nudged by curiosity, Maggie went to the curtained doors and peeked out.

"The gardens are out past the porch," Cole said, coming to join her.

"Gardens?"

"Catherine, Kirsten's mother, initiated the gardens. They've been somewhat neglected this past season with Catherine away," he admitted. "But I did my part and kept the vegetable patch up."

Maggie's thoughts were spinning with new impressions. A mental image of Cole's strong, well-shaped hands grimy from working in a vegetable patch came unbidden. And, she wondered, what had become of this Catherine, Kirsten's mother, Cole's stepmother?

"I guess I could give you a tour," Cole was saying as he chose a chair and sat down rather gingerly. "But to tell the truth, I'm about done in."

Curiosity forgotten, Maggie formed an apology. "I wasn't thinking! You must be exhausted. Why don't you let me help you to bed?"

"No, I had enough of that at the hospital." Eyes sparking mirth, he added, "From here on out, I'm striving to create an impression far removed from the ailing patient in need of a soft touch, a sympathetic smile."

Careful not to inquire what impression that might be, Maggie insisted, "At least let me take your jacket. And why don't you kick off your shoes and get comfortable?" Without awaiting his reply, Maggie unlaced his shoes and pushed the hassock into position.

His voice rang with laughter. "Careful. Fetch my slippers and the paper, and I'll keep you around for a house pet."

Pulse quickening at the warmth of his voice, Maggie said, "I should be going. Shall I summon your housekeeper first?"

"Don't rush off yet," he said. "Sit down and talk to me."

"I have to go." Maggie edged toward the door. "I have to find a way to tell my brothers I lost my job. I have a feeling they'll give me the old horse laugh. They were all against my taking the job in the first place."

"So? Don't tell them," he said. "You're a grown woman, entitled to her own confidences."

"And don't you think they might suspect something when I fail to go to work tomorrow morning?"

He lifted his shoulders in a negligent shrug. "Something else will come along."

"Jobs aren't all that easy to come by these days," Maggie informed him, thinking how easy it was for a man of his wealth to take temporary unemployment as something no more serious than a bothersome fly.

"You haven't even gone and I'm bored," he complained as she continued toward the door.

"I'll call your housekeeper," Maggie offered.

He waved her offer aside. "Birdie is a nice

132

lady, but a little difficult to converse with. You have to repeat everything twice if you don't shout it the first time."

"Then take a nap," Maggie suggested. "You look as if you could use one." Waggling her fingers at him in a farewell gesture, she continued to the foyer and out the door.

How was she going to break the news to James, Justin, and Trent? Maggie wondered all the way home. Justin and Trent would laugh and then most likely forget it. But James wouldn't be satisfied until he'd rubbed a little salt into her wounds.

Maggie was still pondering it as she waited for her brothers to come in for supper. She glanced out the kitchen window and saw Alice's green Vega screech to a halt beneath the pole light.

Alice came whipping up the walk and burst in the door. "Maggie, it's just so unfair!" she burst out. Shrugging out of her jacket, Alice went on. "I admit I had my doubts Nadine would say the things you told me she said yesterday. But now! Well, there's no disputing it!"

Blue eyes flashing war signals, Alice raved on. "Tomorrow morning let's go and see Mr. Dempster. I'll go with you. I'll back you up all the way. You'll get your job back, I'm sure of it."

Maggie shook her throbbing head. "What would be the point? Working with Nadine would be impossible after all that's happened."

"You could change shifts," Alice suggested.

"That would never work out here at home. If I worked nights, the guys would come stamping in expecting breakfast, lunch, and dinner. They'd take full advantage of my being home and never consider I had to have a little sleep."

"Those brothers of yours need whipping into shape!" Alice exclaimed.

Her friend's mouth was set in such a determined line, Maggie could see Alice was considering taking on the job. She chuckled in spite of herself. "Alice, you don't counteract years of spoiling with one stern lecture. Save your breath. They'd only laugh. Especially James."

"We'll see about that!" Alice said forcefully. "Where are they? In the barn?"

Maggie nodded and Alice made a beeline for the door. "They're milking," Maggie warned her. "Cows. Remember?"

Alice's determination dimmed. "Maybe the boys and I'll have our talk after supper," she said with uncertainty.

"This is my problem, Alice. I appreciate your concern, but let me handle it my way," Maggie told her. She stirred the spaghetti sauce on the stove and lowered the burner beneath the spinach.

"Set yourself a place at the table," Maggie told her friend and, as Alice moved to obey, she added, "I haven't told the boys that I got fired, so please don't blurt it out."

"Haven't told them?" Alice gawked at her. "Why ever not?"

You had to really know James and Justin and Trent to realize how insensitive they could be. Reluctant to seem disloyal by shedding the cold light of reality on their less desirable traits, Maggie turned back to the stove, saying, "I haven't had time. They were in the fields today and they went straight to milking without coming in, so I haven't even seen them yet."

"You did come home, then. I heard you picked Cordell up at the hospital this morning. Wondered how you'd spent your day." Alice shot her a wicked grin.

"Don't let your imagination run wild," Maggie murmured. "I'll admit I find him very attractive, but I'm no fool, Alice. He has more women than you have freckles and I'm not going to be just another face in the crowd."

"I think maybe you exaggerate just a little. Anyway," Alice said, pulling out a chair and plunking herself down, "unless I'm mistaken, you're already involved with Cole Cordell — heartwise, anyway."

Maggie tossed a hotpad at her. "If you were half as handy in the kitchen as you are at reading my secrets, you'd win James over, no problem."

Alice said, "Really? Maybe I should take a cooking course." When Maggie's laughter died, she added, "No that's the wrong approach entirely. If I win Jim's interest, it'll be on my own merits. I've no desire to try and fill your shoes. Washing, cleaning, slaving over a hot stove."

"Regular salt mines, it is," Maggie said, but her sarcasm was lost on Alice, for she nodded in sincere agreement. That being Alice's attitude, Maggie didn't think much of her chances with James. He was a farmer first and foremost, and he needed a partner who'd pitch in and help. Of course, there was such a thing as compromise.

Was there any chance James and Alice could each give a little, bend like the willow? Willow. It made Maggie think of Cole and a shot of longing rushed through her. She missed him already and it had been only a few hours since they'd parted company.

136

"Alice?" she ventured casually. "What do you know about Kirsten Fontana's mother?"

"Catherine Cordell? Not much. Why?"

"Oh, Cole mentioned her briefly today. I just wondered what had become of her."

"Seems to me she's turned world traveler," Alice said. "I could ask around."

"It isn't important," Maggie said. "I was just curious."

The door opened and Maggie turned in time to see a light of pleasure steal the weariness from James's face as he spotted Alice. But he only nodded in her direction, then marched off to the bathroom to wash up. Trent and Justin were more vocal in their welcome.

The last of the corn having been harvested, all three men came to the table in festive spirits. Or was Alice the reason behind their good mood? Maggie didn't try to sort it out, only accepted it and tried to be cheered too.

True to her word, Alice made no mention of Maggie's being fired. She did, however, bring up the subject of the girl in radiology who, according to her, was dying to meet Justin.

After his first startled glance, Justin hooded his surprise and accepted Alice's subtle way of discouraging him from thinking further of her in a romantic way. He glanced quickly at Trent, who was looking equally surprised, then up to the head of the table where James was watching Alice with a guarded expression.

Then in his cooperative, cheerful way, Justin queried, "If she's tall, blond, and violet-eyed, what is there to keep us apart?"

Alice was encouraged. She proceeded to get his permission to arrange a blind date. Then she asked, "Shall I see if she had a roommate or a sister, Trent? It might as well be a double date."

Trent's tanned expression fell. He'd mistakenly decided he was the object of Alice's true interest. He mumbled something unintelligible into his spaghetti.

Alice looked to Maggie for help.

"How about you, James?" Maggie said. "Trent doesn't seem too interested in a double date."

It was a toss-up who looked the most outraged, James or Alice. James pushed back from the table and glowered down at her, then at Alice. "What is this — a computer dating service?"

Alice, for once, had lost her tongue. Color washed up to hide her freckles. But Maggie took it with a casual shrug. "Just trying to help."

"Who asked you?" James demanded, then stormed out the door, letting it slam behind him.

"Where's he going?" Alice asked in an alarmed voice.

"To the barn, I suppose," Maggie said.

"I'll go after him." Alice rose and crossed to the door.

"Thought you didn't like cows," Trent put in pettily, and Justin had a chuckle at Alice's expense too.

She tilted her chin at a brave angle. "I don't. But maybe I can learn." Still, she hesitated on the threshold.

"Go on, Alice," Maggie reassured her. "The cows are turned out to pasture after the milking. You're perfectly safe."

Alice smiled her gratitude and slipped out the door. Maggie gave Trent and Justin a pat on the back. "Face it, fellas. She likes the deep, dark, and difficult type."

Justin's laughter rang out. "Fine by me. Say, is this blonde as good looking as Alice says?"

Maggie assured him that she was, omitting the girl hadn't enough personality to fill a thimble. Turning then, she tried to soothe Trent's ego by reminding him of a girl he'd dated in high school.

"I ran into Becca a few days ago. Did I tell

139

you she broke her engagement to the butcher? And she asked about you, Trent."

Trent adopted a stoic face. "Save your blarney, Mag. I'll survive." Trent stalked out of the kitchen. Maggie heard the television blurt on and the couch creak.

"Ah, love's thorns," Justin quipped and, without being asked, helped Maggie clear the table. That chore completed, he joined Trent in the living room, leaving Maggie alone to wash the dishes.

Having tidied up the kitchen, Maggie switched off the kitchen light, then switched it on again as the phone rang. For the second time in one day, Cole Cordell's voice flowed over the wire.

"Maggie?"

Her heart rose to her throat. "Yes?"

"My mind must have been in a holding pattern. I still need a driver. You're available and I wasn't quick enough to realize the beauty of it. Say you'll do it."

"Oh, Cole," she demurred, filled with tantalizing misgivings. "I don't know if that would be very wise."

"Careless driver, are you?" he teased. "Let me worry about that."

No, she despaired. It was more a matter of her careless heart. "It wouldn't work out," she hedged. "The guys need me here."

140

"Then you told them?"

"Not yet. But I'm going to. Alice is here and I haven't had the opportunity."

"Maggie, consider it a moment," he urged her. "The hours can be arranged to your convenience."

She was so sorely tempted. A few more days with him. Yet what was the point? Her heart was bruised at present. Did she want it totally shattered?

"No," she said, though there remained a tone of uncertainty.

"Are you afraid?" Cole challenged.

"Of you? Why would I be? I can hold my own," she claimed.

"Then be here tomorrow morning. Seven o'clock. See you then."

Did that man always have to have the last word? she wondered in exasperation as her good-bye was spoken to a dead line.

In this case, he just *thought* he had the last word! But in the morning, he'd find out differently. Seven o'clock would come and go and Maggie Price would be nowhere near Cole Cordell's grand estate.

Or so she told herself.

CHAPTER TEN

"Aren't you going to be late for work?" James asked the next morning upon coming into the kitchen to find Maggie listlessly staring into a cup of cold coffee.

Maggie rose from the table and poured it down the sink.

"You aren't even in uniform," James noted. "What gives? Did the workaday charm lose its glow?"

Prickly to start with, Maggie didn't need his goading. She spun around and glowered at him. "No, it hasn't lost its glow. I'm running a little late, that's all."

She tore into her room, donned her uniform and, in less time than it took to think it out, was behind the wheel of her car. In her rearview mirror, Maggie caught a glimpse of James watching from the open doorway. A puzzled look lined his face. His intuition be hanged! He wouldn't figure this one out. And Cole was right. She was a grown woman. She didn't have to check with James on her every move.

So what was she going to do? Drive around all day? In this stupid blue uniform, she certainly wasn't dressed for seeking employment.

But there was a job available where her manner of dress would make no difference. Maggie tried to put aside the tempting reminder, as she pulled into a roadside restaurant to let a second cup of coffee grow cold. Try though she did, she could not unsnarl her tangled emotions. In final desperation, she decided to drive to Cole's and take the job on certain conditions, the primary one being she would not get romantically involved. How did she put such a blunt statement to a man like Cole without appearing a conceited fool?

He'd probably laugh and claim it was the furthest thing from his mind. Maybe it was. And then again, maybe it wasn't.

The miles passed quickly. Under an overcast, wind-chilled sky, Maggie steered her car between the opened iron gates at the Cordell estate.

Hesitancy marking each step, Maggie climbed out of her car and took the brick path to the house to ring the bell. Expecting the housekeeper to answer her summons, she felt a panicky last-minute unreadiness when the door opened to frame Cole.

Dark brown hair glistening, clean-shaven and pleasantly scented he set her pulse to racing even before a welcoming smile came to his face.

"You're late," he told her. "For the second day in a row, I thought I'd been stood up."

"A new experience for you, no doubt," she remarked as she stepped inside.

He cocked a dark eyebrow. "Rather a sharp tongue for such an early hour. Was it something I said?"

"A best defense is a good offense," she quipped. "May I speak very plainly?"

"Over breakfast, you may." He hid his amusement behind a formal, "Right this way," and ushered Maggie through the house to the kitchen in the rear. It was a large, no-nonsense room meant for food preparation, not dining. Yet a small table was set up in one out-of-the-way corner and it was laid out for breakfast.

"Birdie?" Cole's deep voice rumbled. "Birdie?"

A big-boned homely woman turned from the sink. Her face creased into a smile.

"I thought I heard voices," she said, coming toward them. "And who might this be?" She bobbed her gray head toward Maggie.

"This is Maggie Price," Cole said. "She's going to be my driver."

The woman held her head to one side and surveyed Maggie. "You're a nurse, I see." She took Maggie's light blue pant-suit into account, applying logic where her hearing had failed. "What'd you say her name was?"

"Maggie." Cole raised his voice. "Maggie Price. And she's going to be my driver."

"She's staying for lunch?" Birdie asked.

"No . . . er, yes, that too. But she's my *driver*." Cole had spoken loudly and clearly.

But it was a lost cause. Birdie beamed. "I for one will be glad to have her stay for dinner. We need a new face around here. And such a pretty one!" Birdie ran an approving glance over Maggie.

"Farm girl, I reckon. She has that sensible look. And he needs a sensible nurse, missy. He isn't behaving at all proper for a man just out of the hospital. You'll take him in hand, I reckon." She shook an accusing finger at Cole and he grinned.

"I'm his *driver*," Maggie said in a very loud voice.

"Give it up," Cole suggested. "Birdie's happy thinking you're going to administer sound medical advice. Would you like coffee?"

Having had her quota for the morning, Maggie declined, but joined him at the small round table.

145

"Now," Cole began, halfway into his breakfast. "What was it you wished to be plain-spoken about?"

Maggie cast a glance across the kitchen. Birdie was very hard of hearing, it was true. Still, her presence inhibited Maggie. She tried to say those blunt words she'd been framing in her mind. "I — well, I may agree to this job until something else comes along. But only on certain conditions," she warned.

Cole said, "Name them and we'll negotiate."

"No, we won't negotiate," Maggie told him, remaining aloof despite the color mounting in her cheeks. "It's about yesterday. Remember? As we drove here from the hospital."

"That was a long time ago." Mischief gleaming from his eyes, he helped her not at all. "Refresh my memory."

"You said you would not be so easily eluded if it weren't for your . . . incapacitated state," Maggie managed with difficulty.

"So that's it." He threw back his head and laughed. "Let me assure you, I intend to mend very quickly."

Maggie scraped her chair back. "That's what I'm afraid of."

146

"Are you really?" he taunted in fun.

"Okay, that's it. I'm going. You can find someone else for this job." She propelled herself out of the chair and took flight.

"Wait a minute, Maggie," Cole called after her. "I was only kidding."

Maggie lost her way, had to back out of one room in confusion, then get her bearings before hurrying on to the front door.

"Maggie!" he called again, and she turned to see him striving to overtake her. Heart contracting lest he injure himself moving around so actively, Maggie stopped at the door.

"I *was* only teasing. I know you're a nice girl. And I know you think I'm a dangerous Romeo with strange attachments to a dozen or more women. Though I might take issue with you on that point, I don't think the less of you for being cautious."

Though his mouth was perfectly straight, Maggie thought she detected a trace of humor still hovering in the depths of his eyes.

Hating it that he should laugh at her, Maggie drew herself up haughtily. "I have these three brothers —"

"Who wouldn't hesitate to pound me into the next universe should I harm one hair on that curly head of yours," he finished for her. "I know. And believe me when I say I'm a man of conviction. And I'm convicted of my foolhardy attempt to romance you yesterday. I'm sorry. Satisfied?"

Not really, she wasn't. He didn't look nearly contrite enough to suit her.

"Come on, Maggie, have a heart here." He went on, persuasion in every word. "I'm used to high-pressure days. Hurry, hurry, hurry. And now I have six or eight weeks of complete boredom stretching out in front of me.

"We're in the heart of tourist country. The dells to the north of us, I haven't seen in years. And there's the caves, that Norwegian village, and other things. But I need a driver, at least for a week or two. Say you'll do it and I'll quit teasing you. Is it a deal?"

Eventually, his masterful powers of persuasion won her over. But even as she sealed the arrangement with a handshake, Maggie doubted the wisdom of it.

The morning trickled by, Cole behaving like the perfect host. At his insistence, Maggie followed him up the stairs to wander through the mini-museum which housed memorabilia. He told her the story of the Cordell Harvester, Inc. beginnings, a rags-to-riches story of the enterprising senior Coleman Cordell.

Cole spoke of his father with a fondness, marked by a quiet pride in the man his father had been more than the empire he had created. Later, over lunch, Maggie inquired about Cole's stepmother.

"Kirsten's mother?" Cole swallowed a bite of the hearty thick soup Birdie had prepared. "Oh, Catherine is rather a character. She's flighty, I'm afraid, and a bit self-important, but charmingly so. She isn't at all work-oriented like my father, or even Kirsten, for that matter. She is attractive and fond of a good time. But most important, Catherine was good for my father."

Cole paused, took another swallow of soup, then went on. "Kirsten and I both were grown when my father and Catherine married. Still, Dad was crazy about Kirsten. She was the daughter he'd always wanted. And Catherine filled a void in his life too with her impulsive love of adventure. That's a quality she's maintained, even though Dad is gone now.

"She is off on a tour of the Orient, traveling on the allowance Dad left her, without a worry of squandering it all away. Which is probably what she'll do."

"Then what will become of her?" Maggie asked.

The question seemed to Cole to have an

obvious answer. "Why, Kirsten and I both are well able to provide for her until her next year's check comes."

"Will she return here to live?" Maggie asked.

Cole looked doubtful. "It isn't likely. She comes for brief visits, and her room is always kept ready. But the truth is, Catherine never loved this place."

"And you and Kirsten do?"

He thought that over a minute, then said, "I like it very much, but I'm not possessed by it."

That seemed an odd way to put it, and it prompted another question from Maggie. "Is Kirsten? Possessed by it, I mean?"

"Kirsten has her apartment in Madison, though she keeps a room here too. She throws a party here for her business associates once in a while. Extravaganzas that run almost embarrassingly to extremes."

He gave a short laugh. "I sometimes wonder how pleased Dad would be about that. He built the place as a retreat from a hectic business life. His own entertaining was limited to inviting a few old friends in for dinner."

Maggie had the impression he'd purposely strayed off course. As she ate her lunch, she wondered again, what was his

150

true feeling for Kirsten? He had a way of putting her down with a compliment. Wasn't one supposed to see his beloved in a rosy glow of perfection?

After lunch, Cole disappeared into the only downstairs bedroom to rest, having given Maggie an invitation to explore the house on her own. It was a delightful structure, boasting oddly shaped high-ceilinged rooms, each decorated in its own charming way.

Upstairs, while wandering through the mini-museum at her own slow pace, Maggie encountered Birdie doing some dusting.

"Exploring?" the older woman asked with a pleasant smile, and Maggie nodded. Chatting like a tour guide, Birdie showed her the rest of the upstairs.

"This room is Kirsten's," Birdie said, throwing a door open to a room of pristine white. Only a black satin spread and matching drapes interrupted the impression of spotless white. Birdie did not stray over the threshold. "She hasn't stayed but a night or two since her mother left," Birdie said as she closed the door and proceeded on to the next room.

Throwing open the door on what had been Coleman and Catherine's room, Birdie said, "No one has stayed in this room since Catherine left for the Orient. But I keep it dusted and ready. With Catherine, you never know. She could pop in at any moment for a short stay."

Gathering an impression of dark furnishings and heavy wine-colored drapes and spread, Maggie listened to the housekeeper ramble on.

"That Kirsten and Catherine were poured from the same mold. Both pretended to love this place when Coleman was still alive. But he was scarcely cold in the grave when Catherine found herself another man and tramped halfway across the world with him. And Kirsten, disappointed she hadn't wormed far enough into Coleman's graces to get the house *and* the main manufacturing plant, besides the small implement factory Coleman left her, hightailed it off into Madison and got herself a fancy apartment."

"So Catherine remarried!" Maggie said and wondered, as the housekeeper pulled the door closed, why Cole hadn't mentioned it.

"Married?" Birdie cocked her head and looked at Maggie closely to make certain she'd heard her correctly. "Who said anything about Royce Heatroll being her husband? Catherine's too wily to marry him and lose the allowance Coleman left her in his will." Birdie cackled pure satisfaction, then added, "Coleman knew Catherine pretty well, it turned out. He made provision for her only as long as she remained Mrs. Coleman Cordell."

Maggie didn't trust herself to comment on such a touchy subject. She just trailed behind Birdie until the woman threw open another door.

"This is Cole's suite, though I traded him until he can handle the stairs a half dozen times a day again." An affectionate smile crossed the weathered face.

"Cole's a jewel, isn't he?" Birdie stated. "Not many men of his importance would trade suites with the housekeeper. I think he knew I wouldn't like staying in Kirsten or Catherine's room," she added confidentially.

Maggie's feet were soundless as they followed Birdie into the plushly carpeted room. The suite consisted of a sitting room, bedroom, and bath. The earth tones were tranquil and welcoming. Potted plants and colorful nature paintings lent a cheering touch.

"Cole did the decorating himself." Birdie beamed proudly.

"He shows excellent taste," Maggie said

and by repeating it twice, made herself heard.

Birdie bobbed her head. "Except in women," she added, and for a brief second, her face clouded. "I worry about him sometimes. That Kirsten's a wily one." Just as quickly, her cheerful countenance returned as she added, "Then again, perhaps he knows what he's about."

Smoothing her flowered dress down over her generous hips, Birdie suggested, "Let's go downstairs and have a cup of tea and a cookie or two. I always take a break about now."

Over the tea and cookies, Maggie found conversing with Birdie as difficult as Cole had predicted. The woman was so very hard of hearing, it was necessary to shout to be heard. She wasn't too surprised when Cole wandered in looking as if he'd been awakened from a sound sleep. Who could sleep through her noisy conversation with Birdie?

"I hope we didn't awaken you," Maggie said guiltily, and he grinned, helping himself to a handful of cookies.

"You did, but it's all right. I'm rested and ready to be entertained."

Maggie couldn't help smiling. She'd come to suspect that her role of driver was a hoax. A day home from the hospital, Cole was in no shape to ride around the state sightseeing.

"I think you've mislabeled me," she told him. "Entertainment director might be more suitable."

He laughed and held out a hand. "Guilty as charged. And now that it's out in the open, put your nose to the grindstone and entertain me."

At his insistence, Maggie followed him outdoors. He laughed away her worries that under the overcast, cool day, he'd catch a chill.

Leading her to the garage, he ordered her, "Start earning your pay. Let's go for a ride."

Taking note of several expensive-model cars, gardening equipment, and other odds and ends, Maggie followed him to the far side of the garage. He pushed a button and one overhead door lifted.

He indicated a golf cart, saying, "If you think you can handle all this power, we'll use this for wheels today."

Laughing, Maggie climbed into the cart and awaited instructions. It was a simple gadget.

"No brakes?" Maggie questioned.

Cole shook his head. "It doesn't go fast enough to need them. We won't win the Indianapolis 500, but we won't wear out our shoe leather either."

Maggie steered the cart out of the garage, asking, "Where shall we go?"

"Cut a path across the yard if you like," Cole replied, but Maggie chose not to. Rather she kept to the paved drive, and even then she made it a short ride.

"End of the road," she told Cole, pulling into the garage again.

"Hey!" he objected and grinned. "I'm the boss and you're the driver, remember?"

"Birdie doesn't think so," Maggie countered. "She thinks I'm your nurse. And as such, I say you've been jostled around enough for one day."

Apparently he'd had enough of it himself, for he followed her back to the veranda without argument. By silent consent, they settled into padded wicker chairs. Despite the hazy, overcast sky, the scenery, flush with autumn color, was pleasant to behold.

"Dad tried to save as many of the trees as possible when he had the house built," Cole mentioned at random. "He was a great one for trees."

"Would I be mistaken in guessing you have a fondness for them too?" Maggie asked.

With a grin, Cole confessed that he did. He spoke further of his father, then questioned her about her own family.

Maggie found him a good listener. Warm and content in his company, she felt an unwarranted bit of irritation when a small dark car came up the drive and interrupted their conversation.

Cole shot an anxious glance at the car, then muttered something unintelligible under his breath.

"Kirsten?" Maggie asked.

Cole shook his head, but offered nothing. He rose from his chair, then descended the porch steps to meet a petite young woman as she climbed out of the dark car. Other than her slender, shapely figure, it was her hair that caught Maggie's attention. It was long and lustrous and gorgeously red. For no reason at all, Maggie recalled a snide remark Kirsten had made about Cole having a weakness for redheads. She knew without being told who the woman must be.

They were a fair distance from her, their voices a low murmur. But the woman became agitated and increased volume made it hard for Maggie not to overhear snatches and phrases of their exchange. The harder she tried not to listen, the more distinct the woman's words seemed to become.

Maggie was about to discreetly disappear inside when the redhead's anguished cry,

"Please, Cole! I'm begging you!" nailed her to her seat. Good manners forgotten, Maggie stopped trying not to listen.

"I can't go on this way," the distraught woman cried. "We've both made mistakes. But I want to give it another chance. What we felt for one another is not completely, irrevocably dead. At least, for me it isn't."

Maggie straightened in her chair, tense, listening. The woman's tone fell to a low, inaudible whisper, only to rise again seconds later.

"I thought I could count on you!" she accused. "I trusted you to understand!" Tears in her eyes, the woman whirled around and ran for her car.

Cole was climbing the veranda steps when the woman flung her last words of reproach at him. "Someday, someday soon! I pray life stops smiling down on the mighty Cole Cordell. I hope to heaven you go looking for a friend, one of those old friends you've so heartlessly flung aside, and I hope you get just what you deserve!"

The woman slammed her car door hard. With a squeal of tires, she turned and disappeared down the drive.

Cole looked down at Maggie, and she up at him. An awkward silence stretched on and on until Maggie broke it, venturing, "A temper to go with red hair, I'd say."

Cole sat down, sighing. "Nasty business."

"I dare say Wade Perkins would consider it so too," Maggie said.

"You don't understand," Cole objected.

"Perhaps I do. More than you care to know," Maggie retorted airily. "Wade Perkins's motives to wish you ill become more clear all the time."

"Don't be stupid, Maggie," Cole said brusquely. "You have the wrong idea."

"It hardly matters." Maggie stood up. "It's time for me to go home."

He lay a delaying hand on her arm. "You'll be back in the morning?"

"But of course." Maggie removed his hand from her arm and edged toward the steps. "We have our own arrangement here. Remember? Your complicated love life is none of my concern."

CHAPTER ELEVEN

Passing up any small opportunity given to admit the truth to her brothers, Maggie dressed in her pale-blue uniform the next morning and left the house, her brothers just assuming she was going to the hospital.

It was not a charade Maggie enjoyed. She simply wasn't up to the hard time she knew they'd give her. It was another gloomy, overcast day and Maggie thought with a heavy heart that it matched her spirits. On the way to Cole's house, she likened herself to a child who, after suspecting the truth for some time, learned for certain there was no Santa Claus.

That was how she felt about Cole — let down, disappointed. She could not go on blindly believing he was the conscientious, trustworthy, wonderful man she'd conjured up in her mind. Not when the man's past — maybe even his present — indicated otherwise.

Releasing a soul-weary sigh, Maggie parked beneath a low-hanging oak tree and walked up the brick path. Cole met her at the door, a warm welcome on his lips as he insisted she eat a bite of breakfast with him. She knew herself to be rather glum company for a man who was bending over backwards being charming, yet she simply could not let go and trust her instincts, not about Cole, at least. Not with Rhoda Perkins's pleas still ringing in her ears.

After breakfast, Cole suggested a walk. The chill to the wind would have been less noticeable if they'd been able to set a more brisk pace.

A crisp autumn scent emanated from the fallen leaves as they shuffled through them, moving away from the house.

"A blanket for the wildflowers," Cole said, reaching for a responding smile. He got none. "We wouldn't want them to catch cold when the winter snows blow." He took her hand and swung it in his.

Maggie very pointedly removed her hand from his.

"The autumn is my favorite season," Cole said. "And yours?"

Maggie shrugged, refusing to look at him.

He made a noise of sheer exasperation. "You're really in a foul mood, Maggie. Would you care to talk about it?"

"Not really."

"Well, I do." He jerked her to a halt, all traces of humor gone from his face.

Glowering down at her, he said in a voice oddly hurt, "I awoke eager to face the day, fully expecting to enjoy myself. So far that hasn't happened."

"So you aren't enjoying the day!" she snapped back at him. "Is that my fault?"

"Yes, it is your fault!"

"Then let me say that I *am not sorry*," Maggie said, the force of her temper backing up her words. "I do not care if you enjoy today, tomorrow, or any other day."

He narrowed his eyes and accused, "You're mad about yesterday, about Rhoda's visit."

"Why ever would I be mad? Why would I even care?"

Ignoring her sarcasm, Cole latched onto her arm as she tried to brush past him. "You tell me."

"Let go. You're hurting me."

His hold slackened, but he did not release her. "You're mad about Rhoda and you don't begin to understand. Why don't you just ask me what it was all about instead of putting on this childish display of temper."

Pierced by his criticism, Maggie blurted out, "I'm not mad. I'm disappointed. Disappointed because I thought you were a gentleman. That you had more scruples than to fire a man because you were interested in his wife, who just happened to be an old girlfriend."

"It isn't that way, Maggie." A beseeching gaze traveled over her face. "Rhoda was a long time ago, high-school days. A cherry Coke after basketball games. Senior prom. We've remained in touch, but there has been nothing between us."

"I heard her, Cole," Maggie said. "A woman doesn't shriek at a casual friend from long ago the way she shrieked at you! She doesn't cry and beg in desperation."

"She was desperate, yes," he said evenly. "But not for the reason you've obviously drawn. I fired her husband because he was selling confidential information about Cordell to a rival company. I didn't have any choice. His inability to find another job caused problems in their marriage. So Rhoda came to me pleading that I rehire him. She wants her husband back, but she knows it won't work out until he finds work."

Maggie compressed her lips, unwilling to meet his calm, open gaze.

"Rhoda came to the hospital the morning of my surgery," Cole went on. "She asked me to put Wade back on in the same position he'd left. Wade had never told her the reason he'd been fired. And I didn't want to tell her. So naturally she couldn't understand why I, an old friend, could be so seemingly hardhearted about it.

"Yesterday she came to me again, this time pleading that I give Wade a job of lesser importance. Any kind of a job, just so she could work out a reconciliation in her marriage. When I told her there was no place for him at Cordell's, she flew into a rage. I guess I should have come out and told her the reason I'd fired Wade. But I couldn't. She was already so humiliated at having come to me for help a second time. I didn't want to take away her last shred of pride by telling her her husband is a thief and a cheat. She may suspect it anyway. But she didn't need to hear it from me."

Cole dropped her arm. Benumbed by the magnitude of her misjudgment, Maggie walked on a few steps, then stopped. What an absolute idiot she'd been! Never once had she connected Rhoda's tortured words with the woman's estranged husband! She'd been so quick, so willing to think the worst of Cole. And why? Because she'd decided, all on her own, that he moved in a sophisticated social circle whose values were not her own. How very smug and righteous she'd been! Drawing a short, sharp breath, she turned and made no attempt to hide her feelings of wretchedness.

"I'm sorry," was all she could squeeze past the lump in her throat.

A flicker of relief chased the somber intensity from Cole's expression. "You should be. We've wasted most of the morning with you giving me the silent treatment."

Maggie felt quick color mount her cheeks. "I misunderstood."

"You took me for a cad," he accused. "I should be much more insulted than I am. But since you and I are such short acquaintances, I'm willing to overlook your misjudgment. So what do you say? Shall we forget the whole thing?"

He was so charmingly forgiving! With a rush of warm feeling, Maggie lifted her chin and smiled into his gray eyes. "I'd like that."

They turned back toward the house, the crunch of leaves beneath their feet a pleasant whisper. A mischievous twinkle hit Cole's eyes.

"Before we forget it completely, let me say I'm flattered you apparently thought enough of me to be disappointed." Without warning, as if on a whim, he kissed her lightly and grinned.

"Want to race me to the house for that kiss? You win, you can keep it. Lose and you have to give it back."

"It sounds like a dangerous gamble," Maggie said, her heart racing. "We'd better just walk."

He took her hand and she did not draw it away. It was a warm, comforting feeling. Forgetting her resolve to bury the topic of Rhoda, Maggie asked, "Was Rhoda mad the day she left the hospital too?"

"She does have a temper. And, yes, it did surface that day," Cole admitted. "Why?"

"I was wondering if she was angry enough to fool with your chart."

Frankly puzzled, he asked, "Are you still worrying over that shot of penicillin?"

"Aren't you?" Maggie asked.

"I'm not letting it keep me awake nights."

"Maybe you should."

He seemed peeved at her persistence. "Not so long ago you were positive Wade was responsible for the changes on my chart."

"I know. But I'm considering all possibilities."

"I think you can rule out Rhoda," he said. "Anyway, stop worrying. The danger is past. I'm home among friends. What could happen?"

The range of possibilities seemed limitless, providing someone out there still harbored a grudge against him. Involuntarily Maggie shivered.

He squeezed her hand. "You're cold. Come on. We're almost there."

It wasn't the brisk air that gave Maggie the chills. It was an inexplicable apprehension that Cole was making too little of the incident in the hospital. Yet if he refused to take it to heart, what could she do?

Once back in the house, Cole lazed in a lounge chair on the veranda, refusing to go inside. He did allow Maggie to tuck a blanket around him, and, despite his claims to the contrary, she could see the walk had tired him. Maggie sat quietly beside him until his eyes closed.

Thinking a little activity would ward off the autumn chill, Maggie went in search of a rake. Finding one in the garage, she began raking the front yard. Using the small rake was like trying to empty a big lake with a teacup, she thought, a smile curling her lips. Yet it was a pleasant way to pass time. It seemed imperative she keep busy lest her overactive thoughts catch up with her.

Even so occupied, Maggie could not keep thoughts of Kirsten at bay. She'd clearly been wrong about Rhoda. But it was an established fact that Cole was engaged to Kirsten. Still, they weren't married yet. So was it such a crime, his show of interest, his warm hand holding hers, his glance lightly caressing, a kiss on a whim?

The slam of a car door intruded into her thoughts. Maggie turned and thought, Speak of the devil, for Kirsten, accompanied by an older woman, was coming up the brick walk.

Spotting Maggie, Kirsten changed course and cut across the yard, a pouting sort of frown spoiling her attractive face. The older woman shot a glance in Maggie's direction, then — appearing strangely uncomfortable — hurried on toward the house.

"I take it the yard boy quit," Kirsten said. "But I can't believe Cole would hire a girl for this kind of work."

Maggie felt a quick rise of temper. "I beg your pardon?"

"He obviously isn't giving you much direction," Kirsten continued. "You'll never get this yard free of leaves with that rake." She heaved a disgusted sigh. "Honestly, Cole exercises absolutely no supervision over his domestic help."

Resentment bubbled to a full boil, but before Maggie could formulate a curt reply, Cole was down the steps and crossing the yard. Leaving the explaining to him, Maggie resumed her raking.

Puzzlement brought Kirsten's full red mouth downward. "Say, aren't you the girl from the hospital? The aide?"

"Assistant," Maggie corrected her.

Kirsten gaped at her. "Don't tell me Cole's hired you as a nurse! Why, you have no training!"

"I'm just keeping her around for company," Cole said. He winked at Maggie as he came up behind Kirsten.

Kirsten spun around. "If you were that hard up for company, you should have called me. I'd have taken a day or so off work."

"Out of sight, out of mind," Cole said, mouth twisting into a careless smile. "You know how it is, Kirsten."

"Cole, really," Kirsten scolded peevishly. "You'll give the girl the wrong idea." She linked an arm through his and flashed a tight possessive smile. "You aren't still put out over my desertion at the hospital, are you? Had I known you were going to be so childish about it, I'd have kept faithful watch at your bedside."

"You have a company to run, Kirsten. I understand perfectly."

But Kirsten was not done with explanations. "And then there was that stupid mix-up. You know I have a low tolerance level

169

for stupidity. Especially on a professional level. Had I stayed around much longer, I'd have given them a piece of my mind."

Which she could ill afford, thought Maggie, bristling with hostility.

"I'm not at all sure the hospital was at fault," Cole said, then let it go at that.

Kirsten looked about to argue the point. Her brown eyes sparked displeasure, but rather than indulging in fault-finding with the hospital, she made Maggie the object of her ill temper.

"If the girl's on the payroll, for heaven sake, make proper use of her time, Cole. Why is she raking? Where is the garden tractor and leaf blower?" she demanded.

Cole shot her a pained look. "You ruin all my fun, Kirsten. I was enjoying watching her from the porch."

Another wink and a warm smile in Maggie's direction darkened Kirsten's mood further. Yet she was cautious not to snap in Cole's direction.

Rather, she forced a pleasant note to her voice, saying, "Mother and I have come out to have lunch with you. Did Birdie alert you?"

"No," Cole replied. "But that's all right."

"I don't know why you keep that woman on," Kirsten fumed. "The phone rang at least ten times before she answered it and then I had to scream to be heard. I don't know how you put up with that."

"Why, Birdie's the light of my life," Cole told her. "Didn't you know?"

Maggie's amused smile did not escape Kirsten's notice. With a guiding hand on Cole's arm, Kirsten tossed her head and turned toward the house. "We can only stay an hour or so. Then I must get back to the plant. Mother has just returned from the Orient full of amusing stories." Her voice faded as she led Cole away.

Maggie was feeling both put out and left out when, from the porch steps, Cole paused to call, "Hey, Maggie. Soup's on. Come on in."

Kirsten dropped his arm, shot them both a murderous glance, then flounced into the house alone. Cole was still chuckling when Maggie joined him.

"You'd best watch it, Cole Cordell," Maggie warned him. "I think you're on thin ice with your fiancee."

"I deserve to be," he admitted cheerfully, and escorted her inside for lunch.

Lunch was not a pleasant affair. Kirsten made no attempt to be polite to Maggie. And the older woman, who Cole introduced at his stepmother, Catherine Cordell, also seemed to harbor the opinion Maggie was overstepping social boundaries by joining them.

Of average figure, Mrs. Cordell was well-preserved, Maggie thought. She toyed with her food and sent another curious glance in Catherine Cordell's direction. Something about the woman tweaked a memory and she couldn't for the life of her figure out why that should be — she couldn't place her among even the most casual of her acquaintances.

Give her her due, she could have passed for Kirsten's older sister. Her makeup was artfully applied to conceal lines of aging. Not a strand of gray could be found in her coiffed brown hair. Was it a wig? Maggie wondered idly. She decided if it was, it was a good one. Her clothes as well as her carriage denoted wealth untold.

She had a gay, but self-important air that Maggie found nerve-grating. With her tales of travels in the Orient, she kept up a steady monologue. Maggie's relief could not have been more complete than when Kirsten announced it was time for them to leave.

"I'm expected back at the plant by one-thirty." Kirsten patted a napkin to her full-shaped lips. "This entire day has been one long rush and it isn't going to get any better.

There is a dinner party at Senator Brading's tonight, which Mother and I are planning to attend." She sent Cole an artful glance. "I don't suppose you could be persuaded to escort us?"

Cole expressed open amusement at the invitation. "I'm a seriously ill man. Remember?"

"Pooh! You could go if you wanted to. And, after all, not everyone has a senator for a neighbor," Kirsten chided.

"He and I may be neighbors," Cole drawled, "but our politics are worlds apart."

"I think he's a perfect dear," Catherine cooed as she rose from the table.

"I'll tell him you're still recovering from your surgery," Kirsten offered without being asked. "He'll understand."

Cole's grin indicated a total disregard for the senator's understanding. "Suit yourself, Kirsten."

Catherine paused behind Cole's chair and dropped a kiss on top of his dark head. "If it's late, we may come here instead of driving back into Madison tonight. You don't mind, do you, Cole?"

"Of course, he doesn't," Kirsten answered for him. "Hurry, Mother. When the cat's away, the mice will play."

Catherine delayed a moment longer. "I'm glad we've had a chance to visit, Cole. I'm leaving for a Caribbean cruise very shortly. But, of course, I'll return in plenty of time for the wedding."

Maggie's heart contracted. Rising with excuses of helping Birdie with the dishes, she escaped to the kitchen. Birdie was not in evidence.

Maggie tied the housekeeper's apron around her waist and drew a sinkful of water. She turned as a determined click of heels on the linoleum announced Kirsten's advance.

"I'd like a word with you." Hands propped on shapely hips, Kirsten let her brown eyes rake over Maggie.

"Oh?" Maggie said, forcing a casual tone she did not feel.

CHAPTER TWELVE

Kirsten swept her blond tresses over her shoulder as she fixed Maggie with an arrogant stare. "Let me set you straight, Miss Price, if you're thinking Cole is your Cinderella dream come true," she said in a frosty voice. "You're no more than a passing fancy, you with those innocent green eyes and that Orphan Annie mop of curls! You may amuse Cole at a time when he's acutely bored. But take warning. When he is well again, he'll drop you without a qualm."

The beauty of her face obscured by anger, Kirsten continued to storm. "What you seem not to realize is that Cole is no ordinary man. He does not let his heart rule his head. In a word, he's calculating. He wants the same thing out of life his father had and that is to rule an empire, his father's empire. However, his father left a piece of that empire to me.

"While Cole may be acting very independent of me at the moment, he knows I hold the key to the rejoining of his business empire. Thus I'm a sound business venture. We're a good match, Cole and I, for we understand one another completely."

A chill smile marked her parting words. "So while Cole is frivolously toying with your affections, keep in mind, Miss Price, there will be a wedding in December. And have no illusions — it won't be yours!"

Kirsten whirled about and, her warning having ended, sailed from the room on winds of fury. Caught somewhere between outraged indignation and fear Kirsten had hit on the truth, Maggie slung a stack of dishes into the sink of sudsy water, nearly scalding her hands in the process.

"Birdie uses the dishwasher."

Maggie pivoted to find Cole's eyes upon her. A wary expression stole their warmth. "Where is Birdie, anyway?"

Maggie struggled for a calm tone. "She deserted ship before the gale hit."

"Kirsten?" Cole asked in a word and Maggie nodded. "I'm almost afraid to ask what she said."

"Come now," Maggie said crisply. "You're fearless and we both know it."

Untying her apron strings, Cole ordered, "So give it to me straight."

"Verbatim? Or the general context?" Maggie queried, ignoring the fluttery sensation his nearness induced.

"The general context will do."

Maggie hesitated to be frank. However she phrased it, she'd come off looking foolish, for Kirsten had been partially right. She had all morning, maybe even for the past six months, been entertaining Cinderella dreams. They'd seemed harmless enough until most recently when fantasy and reality had become a murky confusion.

"Are you going to tell me?" Cole prompted.

"Kirsten says you're ambitious," Maggie said.

"Not ruthless?" he jested.

"She left that word out. A calculating businessman who is out to regain his empire. That's what she had to say for the most part."

Cole's eyes narrowed as he reached out and brushed a stray strand of curls back from her face. "Why do I have the feeling you're omitting something?"

Heart racing senselessly, Maggie put more distance between them. Ignoring his question, she asked one of her own. "Is she right? Are you anxious to reacquire the plant your father left Kirsten?"

"I'd like to have it, yes," he admitted. "At a fair price. It would make Cordell a more smoothly running enterprise."

"And what do you consider a fair price?" Maggie asked.

His gaze swept over her, faintly puzzled. "In dollars and cents?"

"No. In scruples," Maggie answered in a flash of honest truth. "Would you marry Kirsten to get it?" she added, then was horrified because she'd overstepped all boundaries of their employee-employer relationship. "No! Never mind. Don't answer that. It's none of my business."

Yet her retraction sounded flat to her own ears. She listened, eager to hear him deny it. The silence stretched on endlessly. Maggie lifted her gaze to his face. A look of consternation furrowed his brow.

"I wish I could say Kirsten told you a pack of lies, Maggie," he said finally.

"Then it's true?" Maggie burst out, heart hurting inside her. "You are going to marry Kirsten for the piece of your empire?"

"Was."

His correction passed over Maggie. She flashed hot with scorn. "I suppose it would appear very naive if I were to ask, Do you love her?"

A shake of his head was the answer. "Not in the traditional sense, no."

"That's cold, Mr. Cordell, even for you," Maggie said tonelessly. "It's hard to imagine being sorry for Kirsten, but I think I am."

"No need to be. She was going into it with her eyes wide open," was all he offered in his defense. "It was her suggestion."

Maggie shot him a withering look. Tossing the apron down, she slammed out the kitchen door into the yard beyond. Moving at a slower pace, Cole joined her at the edge of a plowed garden patch.

"You're overreacting, Maggie. What we planned wasn't such a terrible thing. My father made Kirsten feel like a Cordell. She didn't want to give it up. That is why she won't sell the small implement plant to me even though I've offered her a fair price."

"And you can't stand the thought of giving up one small plant?" Maggie flung at him.

"My father founded that plant," he reminded her. "It isn't like I want to gobble up all the competition."

"Don't get logical with me, Cole. Marrying someone for any reason but love is an insult to the institution."

"The statistics aren't in your favor, Maggie," he refuted. "Look at Rhoda and Wade. Thought themselves to be madly in love, got married, and now Rhoda can't live with him and she can't live without him.

And Wade's so jealous for fear she'll look at another man, he can't think straight. They are just one example. I could cite you a dozen more to match."

"And I suppose you think you and Kirsten would get along just beautifully without love?" she said. "Why, it's as plain as the nose on your face it'd be one long power struggle."

She turned sharply away from the scrutiny of his all-seeing gray eyes. "Oh, what's the use? I don't know why I'm wasting my breath arguing the point with you."

"That's an intriguing question." His mouth twisted into a cynical grin. "Why *are* you?"

He gave a laugh of derision and said, as Maggie's face flamed, "See where letting your heart lead gets you, little Maggie Price?"

Maggie tried to brush past him, but his reaction was quick. He grabbed her and held her tantalizing close. "Where are you going?" he asked softly against her ear. "You're the one who started this enlightening discussion of love-marriage versus arranged-marriage."

"Let go," Maggie pleaded on a strangled breath, but he tightened his hold instead.

In a husky voice, he claimed, "It's you

who won't let go, Maggie. You've cast a spell over me, bewitched me with those lovely green eyes and tender mouth. And just when I had my life lined up in such straight order, you come along and upset my applecart. Organized folks such as I don't like having their best-laid plans turn to chaos. And I, for one, am through being a good sport about it."

Maggie struggled to defy him, to deny she felt anything but contempt for him, but his lips sealed his words with a kiss that burned her soul.

He lifted his head. Mouth twisting cynically, he demanded, "and this to you is sane? I'd be far better off giving Kirsten my name and keeping my head on business."

Tears stinging behind lowered lids, Maggie flung back at him, "Then why don't you?"

Cole's laugh was short. "Darned if I know. Maybe before all's said and done, I will."

Fresh fear of rejection fluttering through her, Maggie renewed her struggle to be free of his masterful hold. Yet his grasp on her heart was even stronger than his physical strength, and he kissed her into compliance, kissed her until doubts took flight, kissed her until she wound her arms around the solid shape of him and kissed him back with all the love she possessed. Only then did he relinquish her to a world of reality.

Cupping her face in his hands, he said, his voice somber, "Now we're in the same boat, Maggie. Sort of like a nuclear arms race. You press the right button, you can blow my world to bits." He flashed a warning smile. "But it's nice knowing I've got the power to do the same."

Oh, he had that all right! Quivering from the impact of his kisses, Maggie watched him walk away. She wanted to go after him, throw her arms around him and assure him she'd never in a million years blow his world to bits. She wanted only to be with him, to do him good all the days of her life. And imagine a man like him, seeming so sure, so self-possessed, having the same doubts and fears of rejection that she fought constantly! Seeing him in that vulnerable light blacked out all her worries about his world differing so much from hers. As the door closed behind him, Maggie's feet started moving.

Entering the house through the kitchen, she called his name. Hearing no immediate reply, she moved on through the dining room. The front door chimes sounded and a moment later Cole met her entering the foyer.

"Someone to see you, Maggie," he said, and she stepped past him to see her brother James framed in the doorway.

"James! What are you doing here?" she said.

Her brother's mouth was set in an ominous line. "I might ask you the same thing." He shifted uncomfortably, shot a reproachful glance in Cole's direction, then asked, "Step outside a minute where we can be alone."

Too stunned to argue, Maggie followed him out to the veranda. Unaware the door was still slightly ajar, Maggie rephrased her question. "How did you find me here?"

"You lied to me, Maggie!" James accused. "You lost your job three days ago and you never told me."

Maggie lifted a hand, as if to hold off his anger. "James, don't get all righteous with me," she pleaded in a small voice. "I didn't lie exactly."

"You put on your uniform and pretended to be going to the hospital," he pointed out. "If that isn't lying, I don't know what is!"

"I wanted to tell you, but I just couldn't," she said. "You were so set against the job in the first place. I knew you'd crow about it. And the way my pride was smarting, I didn't want to listen to it."

"So you lied," he said caustically.

Maggie hung her head. Scuffing the toe of her shoe against the veranda floor, she asked, "How did you know I was here?"

"I went to the hospital to take you and Alice to lunch today." He caught Maggie's swift, startled glance and added, "The harvest is over. I thought I'd earned an hour or so off."

"You do," Maggie rushed in eagerly. "Deserve time off, I mean. You work so hard, James."

"Don't butter me up, Mag. I'm pretty sore at you. What are you doing here anyway? And how'd you get fired? Alice was very vague about the whole deal."

In a miserable rush, Maggie explained how her firing had come about. James's face darkened through the telling.

"I'm surely not so rough on you, you couldn't have told me this three days ago."

"You aren't every easy to talk to about things that matter, James," she told him. "None of you boys are. What I want out of life is a big joke to you if it doesn't run according to your wishes."

"The farm is part yours too, Maggie. You should want to see it do well, I'd think," he said.

"I do," Maggie said. "I love it because it's

home. But I don't want to eat, sleep, and breathe it, James."

He said, "I'm sorry I made you feel so bad you had to lie, Maggie. Now get your things and let's go home. This is no place for you."

"There you go again, James!" Maggie cried. "I'm twenty-one years old. Don't I have a right to decide what is and what isn't a place for me?"

He appeared surprised to find her bucking him yet again. "But Maggie," he objected. "This is different. This Cordell character isn't someone for you to get mixed up with! Why, he could buy and sell us fifty times over out of petty cash!"

"I'm just driving for him for a few more days," Maggie murmured, unaware her flushed face gave away much more.

"Driving? That's a flimsy excuse if ever I heard one," James scoffed. "He could hire a driver without a bit of trouble if he really needed one. Don't be stupid. That isn't why he's keeping you around."

Maggie's temper began to rise. "Be careful what you say, James Price. Cole is a very decent human being and I don't care for your implications."

"I'm not implying a thing. I'm *telling* you!" James matched her temper with his own quick flare. "Playing with him is like playing with matches in a hay mow. When he marries, it won't be a simple farm girl, you can rest assured."

"I am not simple!" Maggie thundered back at him. "And who said anything about marriage, anyway? I'm going to drive the man around for a little sightseeing the next few days, that's all."

"No. He's the one who is about to take you for a ride!" James shouted back at her. "Land, you're thick-headed if you can't see that. The rich marry the rich, Mag. Oh, they connive and cheat together like fleas on a hound dog. Now get your things, tell him you're leaving, and let's go."

"I'm my own person, James Price, and I'll come home when I feel like it, so you can just stop bullying me!"

"No, you'll come home right now or you won't come home at all!"

There ensued a dangerous silence, during which Maggie wondered how things had come to this. Too much emotional upheaval had occurred in too short a time.

Hot tears threatening, Maggie said in a voice pitched near hysteria, "Then I guess I won't come home at all, because I'm through taking orders from you."

For one long moment, she expected him to jerk her out to his truck by the hair of her head. Then, his face lost all expression and he turned away. Without a word, he stalked to his truck alone.

Childhood memories of James, her champion, her defender, her beloved oldest brother, churned inside her, weighing down a sore heart. Yet keeping to the Price code of stubbornness, Maggie maintained it was her life and her mistake, if a mistake was being made. He could not take each move down life's path for her.

James's truck roared to life and spit gravel in a rapid departure. Tears blinding her, Maggie turned and ran inside. Too late, she saw Cole waiting for her. She turned her head and made a furtive swipe at hot tears.

"Your brother, I take it?" he questioned.

"James," Maggie said on an escaped sob and without another word went straight into his open arms.

"It seems he left in a huff," he murmured against her hair. In a voice gently amused, he added, "You do have a way of taking on the whole world in one day, Maggie. What was your quarrel with him?"

"I . . . I don't want to talk about it."

"Well, I do." He held her firmly at arm's length. "It must have been some fight to reduce you to tears. You held your own with Kirsten and with me."

"He said I couldn't come home," she sobbed.

"That's a lot of nonsense," he soothed and brushed her hair back from her hot face. "Of course, you can go home. You can go right now if you like."

"You d-don't understand." Maggie fought to control her sobs by drinking in great gulps of air. "I c-can go if I go right now. But if I keep working for you, I can't go home."

"Oh. Oh, I see. He thinks I'm a corrupting influence." He was thoughtful a moment before adding, "Maybe you should do as he says. After all, he is your brother."

Outraged, Maggie gasped, "Why, you're taking his side!"

"No. I'm trying hard to remain impartial."

Maggie failed to see it was a valiant struggle on his part. He merely sounded brusque, uncaring whether she came or went.

"Stay another hour or two, if you like," he suggested. "Straddle the road between independence and rebellion. Then go home."

"I'm not a road straddler." Eyes glinting rebellion, Maggie made up her mind. "I'll not only stay a few hours. I'll stay until you've recovered and have no more need of me. That is, if you don't object," she wavered.

"Don't you think that's a little extreme?" His smile was brimming with heart-turning tenderness. "After all, I don't want you to get ousted from your family for any fault of mine."

"I don't care!" Maggie stuck out a stubborn chin. "James is going to learn once and for all he can't run my life. He'd best be content running his own. And Trent and Justin's, if they are weak enough to let him."

"So be it." Cole betrayed neither pleasure nor displeasure. "If you're set on staying, have a word with Birdie. She'll dust up Kirsten's room for you."

Maggie wasn't too thrilled with that prospect, especially when there remained a chance Kirsten and her mother might return to stay the night. Wouldn't Kirsten love finding her beneath that black satin spread. Still, having voiced her declaration of independence, she wasn't going to back down. Rather, she went in search of Birdie.

CHAPTER THIRTEEN

Birdie was quick to understand Maggie's reluctance to occupy Kirsten's room. Ruddy features radiating welcome, the housekeeper made a suggestion of her own.

"Why don't you stay in Cole's suite with me? The sofa is comfortable. And," she added with a quick smile, "it'll give us a chance to get better acquainted. Of course, you're going to have to learn to shout," she added, laying a hand next to one ear.

Maggie accepted the invitation readily. Later that evening, she learned the shouting wasn't the hard part. The hard part was enduring the ear-splitting volume at which Birdie kept her television.

Her ears were ringing when Birdie finally switched off the television following the ten o'clock news. Legs curled under her, Maggie took a nail file from her handbag. She paused in her nail-shaping from time to time, intrigued by the flash of Birdie's knitting needles.

In fact, there was quite a lot about Birdie in night garb that was well worth a second and third glance. Huge metallic hair rollers made lumps beneath a frilly night cap. She wore a floral robe of bold purple and fluffy slippers, and she was as talkative off duty as on.

Catching Maggie's silent scrutiny, Birdie peered over her reading glasses and smiled brightly. "This is cozy. I'd forgotten what it was like to have company of an evening. Especially pleasant company," she added. "Somehow, I can't picture Kirsten lounging around in one of my old flannel nightgowns, talking girl talk."

Birdie was lonely, Maggie thought, and why wouldn't she be? When Cole was gone, who did she have for company but Bart Davis, the handyman? And he was a tight-mouthed man who kept to himself.

"It is rather fun," Maggie said loudly. "With three brothers to contend with, I get lonesome for girl talk too."

Birdie flashed her a compassionate smile. She seemed to realize Maggie's random mention of her brothers brought pain for she soothed, "Don't worry about those brothers of yours. They'll come around once they realize how hard it is to get along without you."

Maggie sank deeper into a mire of self-pity. Surely she was more to James than someone to cook and clean. "Birdie, did I do the wrong thing?" she blurted out. "Should I have obeyed James and gone home?"

"Whether you did right or wrong is beside the point now," Birdie said. She paused, counted stitches, and went on. "You'll come to no harm here, so relax."

Moodily, Maggie flung the nail file back into her handbag and wandered across the room, Birdie's long flannel gown flapping at her ankles. Picking a faded leaf off a potted geranium, she mused, "Cole must have a green thumb. His plants seem to thrive."

Birdie nodded her enthusiasm. "His vegetable patch was a wonder to behold. We had fresh vegetables coming out our ears all summer. He hired a girl from town to help me do some canning."

A tender vision brought a smile to Maggie's lips. "It's hard to feature Cole toiling away in a garden. He seems so very . . . professional. I'd think he'd consider gardening very mundane."

"Actually, I think it was therapy against the pressures of his days," Birdie said. She wagged her head thoughtfully. "Cole could surpass even my expectations if he ever gets past the 'Work is my life' attitude. His father had the same fault. He thought if you didn't put a good thirteen-hour day in at the factory, then you were shiftless. That was the one good thing Catherine did for Coleman." Birdie looked thoughtful and paused in her knitting.

"She taught Coleman how to relax and have a good time. And I'll have to say this for her — she might be the flighty type, but while Coleman was alive, she settled into a quiet life and tried to be a good wife.

" 'Course he no sooner died than the wander bug bit her again," Birdie went on, disdain creeping into her voice. "But I can't say I was sorry to see her leave. She and Kirsten are difficult to be around if you happen to be female. They both thrive on masculine attention, as well as a social system that contends the hired help ought to stoop and bow."

"I'd noticed that at lunch," Maggie admitted.

"Ah, yes. They did their level best to make you feel insignificant not to mention extremely uncomfortable. And they do it so effortlessly." Birdie removed her eyeglasses and rubbed her tired eyes.

"But it was because they were eaten alive with jealousy and scared too," she confided. "They both could see young Cole was making comparisons and wondering if he hadn't been hasty getting boxed into that

193

engagement with Kirsten."

Birdie flashed an easy grin, amused by Maggie's obvious discomfort. "It isn't going to be an easy fight, Maggie. But Cole's worth it. So don't turn him over to Kirsten without a battle!"

"Birdie!" Maggie admonished, livid with embarrassment. "I won't deny a certain interest. But I'm not going to chase him, for goodness sake."

Birdie cackled. "And here I took you for a bright girl. A girl who really wants a good fella has to do a certain amount of chasing. The art of it is to let him think he's doing the chasing."

Maggie fell back on the sofa and giggled. "You ought to write a love advice column, Birdie. You'd turn this old world around."

Birdie cackled again. Then with a wide yawn, she announced her intentions of calling it a night. It had been a long day and Maggie was more than ready to crawl between the sheets Birdie had spread for her on the sofa.

Accustomed to the familiar night noises of the old farmhouse, Maggie thought this house seemed oddly quiet. Maggie yawned, curled an arm around the pillow Birdie had provided, and relaxed into the yielding couch cushions. From the next room came the low sound of Birdie's even breathing.

Thinking of the older woman's sincere advice on love brought a smile to Maggie's lips. Amusing. But she wasn't going to heed it. Twice today she'd been warned of the futility of letting her interest in Cole go unchecked. Pure selfishness had been at the root of Kirsten's warning. But James's concern had been genuine. He did not think it within the realm of possibility that a man like Cole could be anything but briefly amused by Maggie.

She pondered James's reasoning. Was he right in thinking wealth built an insurmountable wall? That it voided the basic human need for friendship? Companionship? The instinct to love and be loved? Was he right in cautioning her against Cole, or was he suffering from a snob-in-reverse complex?

Maggie yawned again, hugged her pillow close, and drifted off to sleep.

It was a loud clatter that jerked her out of a dead sleep. Disoriented, Maggie gave her head a shake. Where was she that such an unfamiliar sound should awaken her? Groggily, she put her hand out for a lamp switch. Her probing hand sent the lamp crashing to the floor and Maggie rose from the sofa, muttering a sharp word.

She stumbled to her feet and, hampered by the darkness, knocked into a coffee table. Wincing in pain, she rubbed a bumped shin and continued toward the door in an effort to find the overhead light switch.

"Birdie?" Maggie questioned as her nose detected the faint scent of an exquisite cologne. Someone brushed past her. "Birdie?" she cried a second time, much louder.

Heart thundering against her chest, Maggie found the wall switch and flooded the room with light. A quick scan of the room revealed the toppled table lamp. Nothing else seemed amiss.

"Birdie?" An awful hesitancy dogging her steps, Maggie crossed the sitting room. The door to the bedroom was ajar. Gingerly, Maggie gave it a push and it swung open.

The sight of Birdie's body making a large lump beneath the bedcovers gave Maggie an instant wave of relief. Then she saw the shattered remains of a clay pot, dirt, and geraniums strewn from the bedclothes to the carpet.

Swallowing the scream in her throat, Maggie rushed to Birdie's bedside. How still she lay!

"Birdie!" The scream tore loose as Maggie gave the silent housekeeper a shake.

Fragments of dirt and clay slid down the pillow. Birdie's head lobbed to one side. Maggie shut her eyes tight and swallowed her horror. Someone had clobbered poor Birdie with a flowerpot!

Icy fingers felt for a pulse. Relief weakened Maggie's hysteria as she found the woman's pulse to be strong and steady. Maggie chaffed Birdie's hands and face, calling over and over, "Birdie, wake up! What happened? Wake up!"

Who in the world would want to harm Birdie? Maggie's thoughts rushed about in wild circles. Maggie shook Birdie gently, desperate to hear a word, a whisper, even a moan. But Birdie made not a sound. If she didn't come to soon, she'd have to get Cole. Cole!

The thought of him stunned Maggie. She went hot and cold with fear as a startling realization hit home. Birdie was in Cole's bed. The intruder had not intended to harm Birdie, but Cole. Maybe at this very moment, the intruder was . . .

Maggie tore down the steps, wild fears roaring in her ears. In her haste, she lost her footing. The billowing nightgown a further hindrance, she lost her balance and stumbled down a few steps, then caught herself again. With no thought past Cole's safety,

Maggie tore through the house to Birdie's room where Cole had been sleeping since his return from the hospital.

The door was open. A soft light sent a pale beam into the hallway. A figure, cape-shrouded and ominous, blocked the bed and Cole from view. A cold chill crept up Maggie's spine as a hand reached from beneath the cape to take out a crystal goblet.

Containing what? Maggie wondered wildly. The pale light cast such a sinister glow on the dark-caped figure that, even as very ordinary words were spoken, a scream rose in Maggie's throat.

The figure wheeled around. It was Kirsten. Swathed not in a cape but a free-flowing black evening gown, the outraged woman demanded haughtily, "What do you think you're doing, barging in here?"

Solely intent keeping Cole from harm's way, Maggie spoke in a frantic tone. "Don't drink it!" She snatched the glass away.

"It's only water. Have you lost your mind, Maggie?" Cole demanded, then tossed two pills in his mouth.

He reached for the glass. Maggie struggled with him for it, showering both him and the bed in the process. "Spit those pills out, Cole, spit them out!" she cried. "Kirsten's trying to kill you!"

"With aspirin?" he queried, his voice filled with impatience and amusement.

"She *is* crazy. Cole, order this young woman out of here this instant," Kirsten demanded, drawing herself into a tall, slender column of total outrage.

"No, listen!" Maggie cried. "She thought you were upstairs. In your suite. In your bed. But it was Birdie she clobbered. Then realizing her mistake, she came down here. Cole, spit them out! Don't you see? It's been Kirsten all along. She's trying to kill you!"

Cole's amusement faded. He scowled at her. "Maggie, calm down. No one's trying to kill me. And what's all this about Birdie getting clobbered?"

"With a clay flowerpot." Maggie's words tumbled over one another. "Someone — Kirsten maybe — crept into your room and, thinking it was you, smashed a flowerpot over Birdie's head. She's still unconscious. Oh, Cole, do spit out those pills before it's too late. Don't tell me you swallowed them?"

"For the love of Mike!" Kirsten snapped. "You surely aren't going to listen to this dithering idiot. She's obviously been drinking. Or had some wild nightmare."

Reserving his opinion, Cole climbed out

of bed, reached for his robe, and followed Maggie out of the room. "Show me," he said, putting a steadying hand on her elbow.

Kirsten trailed up the stairs behind them, cursing all the way. "If this isn't something. What is this girl doing here, anyway? I thought she was your driver, not your bodyguard."

Cole ignored Kirsten and hurried his steps to keep up with Maggie. The suite was as she'd left it. Only, Birdie was sitting on the side of her bed, gingerly removing hair rollers. She turned bewildered eyes on Maggie and Cole.

"What happened?" she whimpered.

Maggie's temper exploded all over again. Imagine bashing poor Birdie! She pointed an accusing finger at Kirsten. Livid with rage, she exclaimed, "Kirsten clobbered you with that potted geranium, that's what!"

Birdie darted an unsteady glance at Kirsten. Her mouth trembled like the mouth of a child who'd been spanked without cause. "But why would Kirsten want to hurt me?"

"She didn't realize it was you," Maggie said. "It never occurred to her you'd be in Cole's bed."

Kirsten burst into a colorful description of Maggie's lack of mental facilities, ending with an irate order to Cole. "Get that woman out of here! Get her out this minute. I won't abide this . . . this . . . miserable, cheap, wretched little witch undermining your trust in me. I would never harm a hair on Birdie's head. And it goes without saying that only an imbecile would think me capable of hurting you, Cole."

Her face contorting, Kirsten demanded, "Order her out of our house this very minute, Cole!"

Cole said, "*Our* house? You mean *my* house, don't you, Kirsten?"

Kirsten sent Maggie a wilting look of utter malice. "You mean to tell me you believe her? But that's impossible!"

"Stop screeching and let me work this out," Cole commanded, then turned to Birdie. "Are you all right, Birdie? How's the head feel?"

Maggie's deft fingers worked gently over the housekeeper's scalp searching for lumps or cuts.

Birdie winced, saying, "There is a tender spot or two. But I guess those ridiculous hair rollers caught the brunt of it."

"You should see a doctor," Cole began.

But Birdie shook her head, protesting, "Eh?"

"A doctor," Cole shouted.

"No, no." Birdie shook her head vigorously. "No doctors for me. I loathe them one and all."

A worried frown puckered Cole's smooth brow. "Okay. But calm down and try to tell me what happened."

Maggie stood silently by, squeezing Birdie's hand for encouragement. Birdie sent Kirsten a bewildered glance. "It must be like Maggie said. Someone hit me with that potted geranium. But I didn't hear or see a thing. Just woke up with a headache and a bed full of dirt."

Maggie swiveled to face Cole. "Don't you see, Cole? Kirsten intended to kill you, not Birdie. You took those pills she gave you and you haven't the faintest idea but that they weren't —"

Cole clapped a hand over her mouth. "Hush, Maggie. It's not what you think. I don't know what happened here. But Kirsten didn't hit Birdie with that flowerpot and she didn't give me anything but common aspirin."

"But someone ran out of here after bashing Birdie," Maggie insisted. "And down the steps, probably straight to Birdie's room, reasoning you'd be there. It had to be her, Cole. Who else could it be?"

"Mother, perhaps?" Kirsten suggested

sarcastically. "She did come home with me. Shall we get her out of bed and give her the third degree? If she doesn't confess, we'll put the screws to her."

"Shut up, Kirsten." Cole's voice cracked like a whip. "This is nothing to joke about. Whoever was in here could have done Birdie serious harm. Let's go downstairs and call the police. Then we'll get Bart on the house phone and have him start a search of the grounds."

"The police?" Kirsten shuddered delicately. "Do you really think that's necessary? You know how the papers are when they get wind of something like this. They'll blow it all out of proportion. And after all, if Birdie's all right, there was no permanent damage done."

"I'm okay, really I am," Birdie chimed in. "I'd rather you didn't call them myself. What purpose would it serve? I can't tell them a thing."

"Well I can!" Maggie said. "Someone hit Birdie and someone ran past me."

"We'll go downstairs and check the windows and doors," Cole said. "Maybe it was an intruder. If we find evidence of forced entry, we're calling the police."

Uneasy with his reluctance to face that it could just as easily be Kirsten, Maggie trailed Cole down the stairs and through the house. The French doors leading out to the screened-in porch were found to be unlocked, as was the porch door.

"It could be someone came and went by them," Birdie mused. "I don't remember locking them."

"Nor do I," Cole muttered.

"Mother and I used the front door." Kirsten shot Maggie a malicious look. "Being family, we have keys."

Undaunted, Maggie asked, "How long ago did you and your mother come in? Did you lock the door behind you?"

"You don't question me," Kirsten retorted icily. She waved a threatening finger under Maggie's nose. "You are the outsider here. Perhaps someone paid you to leave a door unlocked. Your presence here is very suspicious to me."

Before Maggie could refute her accusations, Cole intervened. "This bickering is accomplishing nothing. Kirsten, you're going to awaken Catherine and you know how incapable she is of handling situations such as these. It's beyond me how she's slept through all this shouting."

"You don't suppose someone has . . ." Kirsten's face blanched. "I'd better go check."

Was her concern feigned or genuine? Maggie wondered as Kirsten rushed toward the stairs. Birdie trailed along behind Kirsten, calling back over her shoulder, "If the excitement is all over, I'm going back to bed."

Maggie made a move toward the steps too, but Cole pulled her back. She looked at him questioningly. "Shouldn't we go with Kirsten to see about her mother?"

"Catherine is fine," he said tersely. "She's taken another of those sleeping pills of hers, I'd imagine." He led her to the nearest sofa saying, "Sit down. I've a quick word to the wise for you."

Maggie turned questioning eyes on him as he lowered his frame beside her and paused, as if choosing his words with great care.

CHAPTER FOURTEEN

"I don't understand you, Cole," Maggie burst out in passionate tones. "I don't believe for a moment Birdie was the intended victim of that flowerpot, nor do you. It's so clear someone made an attempt on your life. Yet you rule out everyone in residence. You let Kirsten talk you out of phoning the police, and you ignore the obvious — that Kirsten probably has a very good reason for her strong objection to police interference!"

Cole lifted a quieting finger to her lips. "Hush, Maggie, and listen. It wasn't Kirsten."

"How can you know that?" she argued heatedly.

"Because she was with me."

"But . . ." Maggie stopped short, her face flooding with warmth. "I see," she said in a hushed, flat voice.

"No you don't see!" A spark of irritation lit Cole's eyes. "Catherine and Kirsten stayed rather late at the senator's, and decided to come here rather than drive into Madison. I heard them enter the kitchen. With Birdie's room so close, it was hard not to hear. They talked the party over between themselves a few moments. Catherine mentioned taking a sleeping tablet, then went off to bed, leaving Kirsten behind to raid the icebox.

"By that time, I was thoroughly awake. So I got up, had a sandwich with Kirsten, and listened to party gossip. I must have complained I'd been feeling a bit of pain, for after I told Kirsten good night and went off to Birdie's room, she came, rapped on the door, and offered me the aspirin and the glass of water."

Cole's face was a study of truthfulness. Still something vague and undefinable nagged at Maggie as his gaze slid away from her to the spiral staircase and back. She drew in her bottom lip, thinking. What was it he wasn't saying?

"When the chips are down, they stick together like fleas on a hound." James's contemptuous warning echoed in her mind. Was that it? Was his story contrived to protect Kirsten? She'd heard no voices, no visiting. Was he lying to protect his family from scandal, willing to risk his own life in the process? It seemed foolish beyond belief, and she'd never taken Cole for a fool.

"You're sure it wasn't . . . it couldn't have been Kirsten?" Maggie asked.

"Of course, I'm sure," he said after a brief pause.

Her mind troubled by doubt and fear, Maggie crept upstairs again. All was quiet except for a quiet snore coming from Birdie's bedroom.

The hours of darkness inched by. Was Cole lying awake too? Listening? Or was he, in that infuriatingly careless fashion of his, sleeping with full confidence no harm could befall a man as invincible as he?

Maggie crept from bed from time to time to check on Birdie. Each time she returned to the sofa, relieved Birdie's even sleep was marked by the steady sound of her breathing.

When dawn at last spread rosy flames across the sky, Maggie went to the window to watch the sunrise. She thought of James and Trent and Justin trekking out to do the milking. Were Trent and Justin wondering what had become of her? How had James explained her failure to come home? She shuddered even to consider what wayward trail his explanation might have taken.

Maggie waited to dress until she heard the stirrings of life in the rooms below. A quick check of Birdie found her resting peacefully. Maggie closed the door softly and descended the staircase.

It was not her intention to eavesdrop, but at the sound of Kirsten and Cole locked in an angry exchange, her steps slowed just before reaching the kitchen threshold. Having no wish to walk into the middle of their quarrel, Maggie backed away from the door, waiting for a more tranquil entry note.

It was long in coming. In the meanwhile, it was difficult not to catch snatches of their argument as their voices rose and fell. One terse sentence from Cole caught Maggie's attention.

"The hospital mix-up caught me off guard, Kirsten, but last night was different."

"Cole, please listen to me!" Kirsten pleaded. "I know it's hard for you to understand, but —"

"No!" Cole ground out. "You listen to me. I'll not be murdered in my own bed, nor will I have members of my household subjected to danger. You have two choices." His tone was rigid, unbending. "I can turn this whole rotten mess over to the police, or —"

"Not that, Cole. Please!" A sob caught in Kirsten's throat. "I c-couldn't bear the humiliation. The reporters! The publicity!"

"Or," Cole continued as if uninterrupted, "we'll arrange some psychiatric sessions and very close supervision."

The hypocrisy of it hit Maggie with jarring force. It was Kirsten! It had been all along. He'd known it last night and constructed that neat lie to protect her. Her blood churned to a slow boil.

If the average man attempted murder, it was a police matter, cut and dried. But if you had wealth? A few sessions with the shrink to unsnarl your hang-ups and presto! You were all better, forgiven, forgotten. Maybe in the end, Cole would still marry her! James was so right. They did stick together like fleas on a hound. Maggie clutched her broken heart, slipped up the stairs to get her jacket and pocketbook, and without even a good-bye to Birdie, drove home.

The quiet of the farmhouse at mid-morning would have been restful had Maggie not been so anxious over James's reaction to her return. While she doubted he'd made good his threat, she knew he wouldn't let things be easy for her.

One look at the kitchen nearly reduced her to tears. The boys hadn't done too well in her absence. The linoleum floor was boot-tracked, the countertop littered with dirty dishes, and the stove was a mess of dribbles and grease splatters.

Her body cried out for sleep, but her tidy nature forbade her to ignore such a mess. So after changing into jeans and an old blouse, Maggie went to work. By noon, the kitchen was fit for human habitation once more. Expecting the boys at any minute, Maggie prepared sandwiches and hot soup.

Trent and Justin came into the house, pretending she'd never been gone. But Maggie caught their exchanged glance of unease.

Weary and on edge, she snapped, "Wipe your feet. I just mopped the floor."

Justin's face creased into a cheerful grin. "Things are back to normal, I see." But he did as she ordered and Trent followed suit.

Turning away from washing his hands at the sink, Trent asked, "Does James know you're back?"

"If he has eyes in his head, he's seen the car."

"He hasn't been in?" Justin asked. At Maggie's head shake, he added, "Be warned. His mood isn't too cheerful. Alice drove out last evening to see you. When James fed her the facts, she tore him up like a paper sack."

Trent chuckled. "It wasn't a pretty sight. James got all red-faced and indignant."

"But what could he say?" Justin snickered. "He was guilty as charged: a tyrant, a chauvinist, an overprotective brother who doesn't know when to let go."

"A big help that Alice is," Maggie grumbled, her dread of facing James growing by leaps and bounds. "He'll toss me out on my ear for sure now. You know how he hates having anyone take *him* to task."

"I think he could use another dose of Alice." Trent straddled his chair. "She might make a decent fellow out of him yet."

"And I think the three of you ought to mind your own business." From the open doorway, James glowered at them. An awkward silence descended as he singled Maggie out with a pointed, "So you're back."

"Yes." Maggie drew a deep breath. "And a good thing for the three of you. The kitchen was a disaster area and the rest of the house doesn't look much better. Don't take another step off that rug, James. Either wipe those boots or take them off."

"She just mopped the floor," Justin chimed in.

James wiped his boots and went to the sink to wash up. "Didn't things work out with your golden boy?"

Maggie winced at his sarcasm as she

ladled out bowls of hot soup. Stiffening her spine, she retorted, "I'd rather not discuss it."

"Can't talk about Alice. Can't discuss Cordell," Justin grumbled and winked at Trent. "May as well eat and go back out to plow."

To Maggie's relief, no further mention of Cole Cordell was made. The meal ended and Justin and Trent departed for the afternoon's work. James lingered at the table. He drained the dregs of coffee from the bottom of his cup, then fixed Maggie with a surprisingly mollified expression.

"I'm glad you're home, Maggie."

Surprise prompted a curt response. "Missed your maid service, huh?"

His color darkened. "I'm not good at pretty words, Maggie. I guess I don't ever say it, but the fact is, the boys and I think you're about the greatest thing going. I was too tough on you and I'm sorry. From here on out, your life is your own. I won't interfere."

The very words she'd longed to hear! The moment was awkward with unexpressed emotion. Only a trite answer would do. "Could I get that down in writing?" Maggie reached for a napkin and a pencil from the counter.

"Don't press your luck," James grumbled as he pushed away from the table.

"I wouldn't dream of it." Maggie rose too and followed him to the door. "By the way. What's this about Alice . . ."

He slammed the door in her face before the question was completed. Maggie's grin faded into compassion. It appeared she and James were in the same broken-down boat — crazy about people who were not crazy about them, or something.

There was no rhyme or reason to love, Maggie decided as she fought off weariness and tackled the housework. At three-thirty, she sat down for a cup of coffee. Sitting up in a straight-backed chair, she was beginning to doze when the sound of a car pulling up to the house snapped her to attention again.

Going to the window, Maggie saw it was Alice, and there was someone with her. Maggie's eyes widened as Nadine Perkins climbed out on the passenger side. Paying a social call? Highly unlikely! What more could this strange day bring? Maggie wondered uneasily as she answered the door.

"So you *are* home!" Alice said. "I called Cordell's and the housekeeper said you'd gone. Is she deaf, or what?" Alice raised her eyebrows expressively. "I had to shout to make myself understood."

"Birdie's hard of hearing, yes," Maggie murmured and looked past Alice to say with some trepidation, "Hello, Nadine. Come on in. There is fresh coffee in the pot."

"None for me," Alice declined. "But Nadine'll have a cup, I expect. She wanted to talk to you in private. Is James around?"

Amused by Alice's eager, darting glance, Maggie hid a smile and replied, "He's mending some fences out by the barn."

Alice's freckled face shaped itself into a cheerful grin. "Is he carrying any deadly weapons on his person? I do believe he's a little put out with me at the moment."

"A pair of pliers is all, I'd imagine."

"Then I'll take my chances," Alice said and, with a laugh, darted back out the door.

An uncomfortable silence reigned as Maggie filled Nadine's coffee cup, then faced her across the table. "Cream or sugar?"

"No. This is fine." Nadine lifted the spoon from the saucer and idly stirred the steaming dark brew.

"How are things at the hospital?" Maggie queried for want of a better beginning.

"I'm not wanting to beat around the bush," Nadine said. "It's just hard for me to get started." Nadine put the spoon aside.

The frost was gone from her eyes, replaced by a plea for understanding. "I came to ask your pardon. What I did to you was unforgivable and, quite frankly, I've been having a tough time living with myself."

Maggie waited wordlessly through Nadine's painful pause.

"I've always prided myself on being a good nurse," Nadine continued with difficulty. "And though I'm a tough supervisor, I've tried to be fair and demand no more of my nurses or assistants than I would do myself.

"In your case, Maggie, I forgot the basic ground rule. I brought my personal problems to work." She lowered her gaze and silently traced the tablecloth pattern with a finger that trembled.

"Wade has been a disappointment to me in many ways. But he is my only child and I love him better than life. I fear I've made him weak by fighting all his battles for him. But believe me when I say I've never before hurt an innocent person to protect Wade. And that's what I did to you. I was so afraid Wade had changed Cole Cordell's chart. I just wasn't thinking straight. My one desperate thought was to protect him from the consequences."

"I guess I can sort of understand that,"

Maggie said. "But Wade, as it turns out, didn't change that chart."

"I know that now," Nadine said. "Cole Cordell called the hospital this morning. He knew an investigation was underway to determine the reasons for the changes on his chart. And he wanted to make certain no one at the hospital was blamed for it."

"That was decent of him," Maggie muttered disagreeably, "considering it was a member of his own family."

Nadine nodded. "So he said. But, Maggie, even if he hadn't called, I would have come to offer you your job back. I couldn't face myself if I didn't."

The offer came unexpectedly and Maggie was stunned. "I'll have to think it over," she said.

"I hope you'll come back." Nadine's words were marked by sincerity. "You were doing a fine job."

Maggie did not commit herself. It was not the kind of decision she wanted to make without careful consideration.

Rather, she offered her hand, saying, "It took courage for you to come here like this, Nadine. I want you to know I admire that. And I hope Wade and his wife can straighten out their difficulties. It must be very hard for you to see him unhappy."

Tears glistened in Nadine's eyes for one brief moment. Then they were gone as she steered the conversation down less personal channels. Sensing Nadine wasn't one to let her guard down and humbly admit a wrong increased Maggie's respect for the woman so much that her recent hard feelings had completely melted by the time the nurse rose to leave. Maggie walked out with her to Alice's car.

"What is keeping Alice?" Nadine wondered.

Maggie pointed in the general direction of the barn. Fence-mending forgotten, James and Alice were carrying on an animated argument. They were too far away to be heard, but Maggie gathered it was in fun, for suddenly without warning James grabbed Alice and lifted her over the fence. Alice shrieked her protest and struggled to be free — but not very hard.

A smile softened Nadine's severe features as they watched James tug Alice toward a grazing cow. Alice squealed and protested and dragged her heels every inch of the way.

"She's afraid of cows," Maggie explained for Nadine's benefit.

"Really?" Nadine arched a thinly plucked brow. "She appears to be having an awfully good time overcoming her fear."

They watched a moment longer, the battle turning into a warm embrace.

Maggie shook her head. "Nothing like the privacy of wide open spaces. And here I thought James was backward."

Nadine reached in and tooted the car horn. James jumped back, appearing abashed. But Alice was smiling.

"Coming!" she called, turned for a last word with James, then sprinted to the fence and handled it with ease.

"Maggie, why don't you come along with us," Alice invited when she reached the car. "I'm dropping Nadine at the hospital to get her car. Then I'm going into Madison to get my hair done. There's a new shop there," she chatted on. "Costs the very earth. But let's face it — I'm worth it." Giggling, Alice leaned nearer and confided, "James and I have a date this evening."

"Alice, I've cleaned house all day and I'm beat," Maggie protested. "I wouldn't be fit company."

That didn't make any difference. Alice was not taking no for an answer. So after a quick shower and a change of clothes, Maggie accompanied them to Bartlett's where Alice dropped Nadine at the parking lot. Then it was on to Madison.

Alice expressed frank curiosity over Maggie's brief stay at Cole Cordell's, but when Maggie remained closemouthed about it, she stopped her questioning and raved on about the new beauty shop in Madison.

"Everybody who is anybody gets their hair done at Godfrey's," Alice confided. "They aren't just *up* on the new styles, they're *making* them. I can't wait to see what they'll do with me."

"It appears to me James likes you just fine the way you are," Maggie said.

Alice laughed gaily. "James opposes change of any kind on general principle, I do believe. But he may change. He may change."

Reasoning with Alice was wasted breath. It washed over Maggie how mismatched she was with James. But Alice was a good, sweet girl at heart, and who was to say she wouldn't make James happy?

With that thought in mind, Maggie dozed, not to awaken until they had reached the city limits of Madison.

CHAPTER FIFTEEN

Godfrey's was all that Alice had promised. Maggie felt out of place, taking a seat in the plush lounge and trying to let the soft background music put her at ease. But Alice appeared at home. She gave Maggie a cheerful wave, then followed her stylist to the rear of the shop for her shampoo and set.

Despite the bustling activity of comings and goings, Maggie relaxed and grew sleepy. The conversational murmur of women's voices combined with the soft music to fade to a low monotone. Maggie leaned her head against the back of the chair. She was only a degree from sleep when a familiar demanding voice forced her eyes open.

"Just a facial and a manicure, please."

Recognizing Catherine Cordell, Maggie straightened in the comfortable chair. Catherine's gaze flicked over Maggie as she passed by, but she offered no greeting, nor did Maggie.

Ushered to a nearby chair, then swathed in plastic covering, Catherine had her back to Maggie. But Maggie had a clear mirror image of her. Try though she did to ignore the woman, some puzzling similarity to a hazy memory kept drawing Maggie's attention back to her.

She studied Catherine's reflection. Her face was framed by the soft towel which kept her hair out of harm's way. As the beautician applied a cleansing lotion, Maggie watched raptly. But it wasn't until Catherine's face was completely free of all makeup and showing her true age that final recognition came.

Mrs. Rollsroyce from the hospital! Maggie jerked upright in the chair and thought hard as the self-important woman's voice droned on and on.

"The Caribbean cruise will be welcome after this rainy spell we've been having. I detest cold, rainy weather, don't you?" Without awaiting the girl's reply, she went on. "My bags are all packed and I'm leaving this evening. I have to catch my flight out of Madison at seven-fifteen."

Mrs. Rolls . . . who? Maggie tried to remember. The name had given her problems even when she'd tended to the woman at the hospital. No wonder Catherine Cordell had plucked a chord of memory!

But why had Catherine been admitted to Bartlett's under an assumed name? Why

Bartlett's at all? She would obviously have been more at home in Madison. And further, why had she led everyone to believe she was out of the country until the day she showed up at Cole's with Kirsten?

Maggie was so tired, clear thinking was a taxing activity. But there had to be some reason for Catherine's strange actions. Imagine her being at the hospital the same time Cole was there, only a couple of rooms down from his. And never letting on to Cole she was there!

Maggie gave in to her active imagination. Could it be the chart? But no. She'd heard Cole and Kirsten settling that matter this morning. Catherine couldn't have had anything to do with that chart. Could she? Maggie couldn't begin to figure it all out. She waited impatiently for Alice to be finished. Each minute seemed a year and, as the time crawled slowly by, she became more and more sure that she should tell Cole about Catherine's odd little intrigue.

Alice finally came, fresh, tight curls framing her pert, freckled face. "What do you think?" she said, patting her new hairdo.

"Fine," Maggie said distractedly. She bounded out of her chair. "Pay and let's get out of here."

Alice's face fell. "You don't think James will like it, do you?"

"Alice!" Maggie urged her toward the register. "Let's go."

Pouting prettily, Alice paid the girl and followed Maggie out of the shop. "Maybe I should go home and wash it out, redo it myself, if you think James won't like it," she said, preoccupied with her hair.

"No, it's fine," Maggie answered shortly. "Listen, Alice," she said, grabbing Alice's arm as they left the sidewalk for the parking lot. "I have to make a phone call. Pick me up there at that corner booth."

Alice asked a question, but Maggie ran on without answering, peeved with herself for not simply phoning Cole earlier. To her dismay, the line was busy. She waited a moment and tried again. It was still giving the busy signal. Maggie was dialing a third time when Alice pulled up to the curb. Still busy. Maggie slammed the phone down and left the booth for Alice's car.

"What on earth is wrong?" Alice demanded. "You're white as a ghost."

"I don't know, Alice. I have this uneasy feeling I ought to be doing something." Maggie faced her friend as they stopped for a traffic light. "Did you recognize the lady in the first chair?"

"I didn't even notice her. Why?"

"She was Rollsroyce from the hospital."

Alice gaped at Maggie blankly, then gave a short laugh. "Oh! Mrs. Heatroll?" she tried, and Maggie nodded. "So what?"

"She's also Catherine Cordell, Cole's stepmother," Maggie said.

"I think you're overtired," Alice remarked with patient tolerance. "You aren't making sense."

"Just drive, Alice. I need to get in touch with Cole. Catherine is flying out of Madison this evening, and before she goes, I think he should know she was not in the Orient at the time of his surgery, but two rooms down from him in Bartlett's."

"You want me to drive out to Cordell's?" Alice's face turned to dismay as Maggie nodded. "But I have to get home and get ready for my date with James!" she protested. "Besides, I think you're making too much of this. It was probably vanity on Mrs. Cordell's part that had her keeping her small surgery a secret. Cosmetic surgery, wasn't it?"

"Two moles," Maggie replied absently. "Take the road to the right there, Alice."

Alice drove blithely along her chartered course, arguing, "I don't have time, Mag. Besides, it'd be a wild goose chase. I'll drive you home and you can get him by phone."

Frustrated by her inability to get Alice to take her seriously, Maggie sat tensely back in her seat and counted the miles home. Once there, she dashed into the house to make her call. To her dismay, no one answered her ring.

Maggie glanced at her watch. It was right at the dinner hour. Where was Cole? Why didn't he answer the phone? Darn that Alice anyway. It would have taken only five minutes or so to have stopped by his house and she would have been spared all this anxiety. She redialed the number and still no one answered her ring. A premonition of trouble growing, Maggie grabbed a heavier coat from her closet and went out to her car. The night air had a silvery chill.

It was a long drive back toward Madison. With each passing mile, Maggie tried to check her mounting sense of foreboding. Cole was fine. Of course he was! He would have a perfectly logical reason for not answering the phone. She was panicky for no reason.

Still, her apprehension gave her no rest. She steered her car beyond the gates, up to the house. Not bothering to knock, Maggie tried the door. It opened beneath her hand.

Without announcing her presence,

Maggie stepped into the foyer. The sound of loud voices drew her toward the spacious living room.

Just beyond the doorway, her body trembling, Kirsten whimpered:

"Mother, you can't do this!"

"Shut up!" Catherine shouted at her. "You always were a sniveling coward. Either help me with this, or you can die with them."

Kirsten recoiled as if she'd been slapped.

Catherine raged, "Do as I say, Kirsten. Get the can of gas from my car. Drench the ropes in gas, then tie them up. We'll leave a cigarette smoldering in the sofa. By the time the fire takes hold, you and I'll be somewhere over Mexico."

"Be sensible, Catherine," came Cole's voice, low and even. "There isn't a chance in a million of your getting away with this. No one is going to believe this house burned down with Birdie, Bart, and me in it. Now put down the gun and let's talk."

"The time for talking was when the contents of your father's will were made known!" came Catherine's icy reply.

Stealthily, Maggie peeked around the door. Catherine stood with her back to the door. Kirsten stood off to one side, while her mother had a handgun aimed at the frightened threesome.

Birdie looked about to faint from fear. Bart, the handyman, had a supporting arm around her.

"Do as I tell you! Get the gasoline!" Catherine raged at her daughter.

Kirsten ran to Cole and cringed against him. "Mother, this is insane. I want no part of it. No amount of money is worth the lives of three people. Don't you see that?"

"It should be *my* money!" Catherine screeched at them all. "Coleman made a fool of me from the grave."

"The will is your reason for this?" Cole sounded incredulous. "I never knew you were dissatisfied with the allowance left you."

"You honestly believed I was so simpleminded that paltry sum would satisfy me?" Catherine's rage crested. "What a fool you must think me to be! Coleman promised he'd leave everything he owned to me. Everything, if I'd but marry him and bring some fun into his miserable existence.

"So we struck a bargain. I married him. I pretended to enjoy this forsaken country hovel. I even endured the help he hired." She glared at Birdie and Bart.

"I hated it, I tell you! But I endured, knowing he was an old man and couldn't

228

live forever. I kept reminding myself as soon as he was gone, I could have all that money to spend on the pleasures I'd been missing, tied down to Coleman Cordell and his mighty empire."

Voice curdled with contempt, Catherine demanded, "And do you know what really killed my soul when they read Coleman's will? He died thinking he'd robbed me of my inheritance as well as my love. That ignorant old man never once suspected I loathed him."

Gloating, she added, "I wish he could be here just for this one moment in time, just so I could tell him, as I kill his only son, how very much I loathed him!"

Face crumbling, Kirsten pressed closer to Cole and whispered hoarsely, "She's mad."

"Mad enough to see you die too Kirsten, if you don't do my bidding," Catherine raved. "No more stalling. Go get that can of gasoline."

Eyes huge pools swimming with terror, Kirsten shook her tawny head. "I c-can't, Mother."

"But you could conspire with him to send me to an asylum for the insane!" Catherine leveled the gun at Kirsten. "I'm giving you one more chance." Pulling a rope from her coat pocket, she ordered, "Tie them up now, Kirsten. You can get the gas then. Now! Do as I say!" she screamed. "Or do you want to be the first to die?"

Catherine tossed the rope to Kirsten and for a fraction of a second the gun was lowered. Cole charged her and, with a startled outcry, Catherine aimed the gun at him. Maggie was already in motion. Just as Catherine's finger squeezed the trigger, Maggie tackled her from behind. There was a sharp outcry of pain and Kirsten's high, hysterical scream as Bart took the stray bullet and slumped to the floor.

Cole wrestled the gun from Catherine, his initial surprise at the sight of Maggie turning to acceptance. "See what you can do for Bart," he ordered. "Birdie, call an ambulance, then the police."

"Not the police!" Kirsten sobbed. "I — I couldn't face everyone knowing how mad Mother is!"

Cole swept Kirsten with a look of scorn, then gave Birdie a nod, saying, "Go on and call, Birdie. How bad is Bart?" he asked of Maggie.

"Just a flesh wound, I think," Maggie said, hands trembling as she examined Bart's left side.

Catherine pulled herself up from the floor. "Kirsten, don't let them call the police. Don't let them send me away." Great sobs of frustration shook her body.

"Mama, you need help," Kirsten managed in a wobbly, tearful voice. "No one will hurt you. I won't let them. Haven't I always protected you?"

Maggie felt an unaccountable wave of compassion as Kirsten went to her mother's side and gathered her close. Riveting her attention back to Bart, she noted he was starting to come around.

"What happened?" he mumbled. "Cole!"

"Shh. Cole's fine," Maggie soothed. "Try to keep still. An ambulance is on the way."

CHAPTER SIXTEEN

After the police had come and gone, Maggie drove Cole to the Madison hospital to make certain Bart had suffered no permanent injury.

It was a swift and silent ride. But once they'd seen Bart and been assured by his doctor that he was only keeping him overnight, the world seemed to slow to a more sane pace.

"Buy you a cup of coffee?" Cole offered, taking Maggie's hand.

The coffee shop was nearly empty. Maggie slid into a booth and Cole sat close beside her. The waitress brought their order, then returned to her flirtation with a young man at the counter.

Cole stirred sugar into his coffee, his gaze long and measuring upon Maggie. "You look dead on your feet," he said.

Maggie stifled a yawn. "I haven't had any sleep and it has been a very strange day. Just about the time I thought I might get some rest, Alice came and dragged me into Madison with her. We ran into Catherine at the beauty shop and, well, from there on, it got very confusing."

"The beauty shop?" Cole questioned. "So that's where she got off to. Kirsten called all over the place when Catherine slipped off, but she couldn't find anyone who'd seen her. Then we went out and searched the grounds. When we came back in, she was waiting for us. Stupid trap for us to walk into, knowing what we knew."

"You mean you knew it was Catherine and not Kirsten trying to kill you?"

Cole replied, "But of course. What did you think?"

"When I overheard you and Kirsten arguing this morning, I thought . . ." Maggie stopped short, her features heating at the realization she'd confessed to her eavesdropping.

"Go on," Cole prompted. A glint of humor enlivened his fine gray eyes. "What did you think?"

"I thought it was Kirsten and that you'd covered for her. You know, over bashing Birdie with the flowerpot. And," she continued with difficulty, not quite daring to meet his eyes, "I thought you were bargaining with her to leave the police out of it if she'd agree to seeing a psychiatrist."

"We were discussing Catherine, not Kirsten," Cole said. "We both realized last night it could be no one but Catherine."

"And did you also realize Catherine was in the hospital at the same time you were?" Maggie questioned.

"Not until I called the hospital early this morning," he admitted. "I asked a few questions and learned that Catherine had checked in under the name of Mrs. Royce Heatroll. They also passed the information along that they'd wanted to do some tests. It seems they suspect she has a brain disorder."

"Which would account for her sudden violence?" Maggie gasped.

Cole nodded solemnly. "That was why I hesitated to make it a police matter. But now the police have her — and she'll get some kind of psychiatric treatment. Catherine left the hospital on her own, without being dismissed. They were very concerned about her."

"And I thought you were covering for her just to protect your family name," Maggie confessed haltingly. "It seemed such a snobbish, hypocritical thing to do . . ." She trailed off into silence.

Cole looked as stricken as if she'd slapped him. "And that's why you left without saying good-bye?"

"I — I'm sorry," she managed haltingly.

"I figured you'd changed your mind and taken your brother's advice," he said softly. "It wasn't going to be that easy to get away from me, though, Maggie. In a day or two — however long I could hold out — I was coming after you."

Maggie got that fluttery sensation in the pit of her stomach as his warm gaze wandered over her. "What about Kirsten?" she had to ask.

"Kirsten was a stupid idea I had once." He leaned nearer, his mouth touching hers in a gentle caress. "I started figuring that out the first time you walked into my hospital room and stole my heart away."

Oblivious to the young couple at the counter, Cole kissed her more thoroughly. "I've had a lot of time to think the last few days," he murmured against her mouth. "And it occurred to me that, though I've had a lot of things go my way in life, there has been an emptiness." He drew a ragged breath. "Will you fill it, Maggie? Will you be my wife?"

Heart overflowing with rapture, Maggie answered him in a lingering kiss that drew a wolf whistle from the young man at the counter.